MW00559018

The Only
Dragon

STEPHEN H. PROVOST

Stephen A. Provost
4-22-23

Dragon Crown Books 2018
All rights reserved.

ISBN: 1-7320632-8-1
ISBN-13: 978-1-7320632-8-0

Dedication

For Puff, wherever you are.

Contents

Thanks

Thanks to Samaire Provost for her invaluable contributions in editing this manuscript.

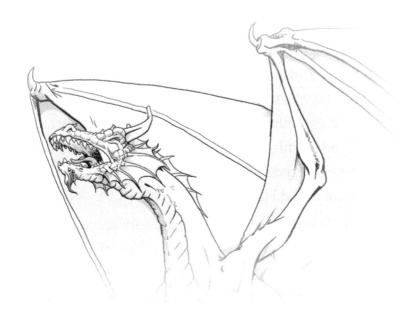

Introduction

 hen I was a toddler, my parents gave me a stuffed blue snake that became my near-constant companion. But to me, he was never a snake. He was a dragon. I named him Puff, after the Peter, Paul & Mary song.

Puff was my friend and protector throughout my childhood. When his plastic eyes came unglued and his red tongue was torn off, my mom made new eyes and a mouth from colorful pieces of felt and sewed them on as replacements. (They looked a lot cooler than the originals, and I'm sure Puff could see more clearly as a result).

Somewhere between my early teens and adulthood, Puff and I went our separate ways. Like many children's companions, he was misplaced or accidentally left behind when I was busy collecting baseball cards, playing intramural basketball and learning how to drive. I suppose, just like his musical namesake, he sadly slipped into his cave in that mystical place called Hanalei.

I later learned that Hanalei wasn't imaginary at all, though — that it was a real town on the Hawai'ian island of Kauai, which I visited with my parents during several summers about the same time Puff went missing. Did he hop off the plane and hitchhike to Hanalei?

I suppose I'll never know. But if Hanalei is a real place, isn't it just possible that dragons are (or were) real themselves? Myths and legends about dragons can be found on opposite sides of the world, from China to Great Britain. They come in various shapes and sizes: winged, fire-breathing, serpentine, with two legs or four ...

How is it that so many similar stories arose so many thousands of miles apart?

Dragons, I noticed, sounded a lot like dinosaurs, another childhood fascination of mine (as they are for so many youngsters). I spent countless hours with a set of plastic dinosaurs, my dad's generation played with toy soldiers. My favorite was the plastic blue ankylosaur, whose armor plating could repel the fiercest predator and which could use its cudgel-shaped tail to beat the tar out of any allosaur stupid enough to get too close (at least in the scripts I wrote in my eight-year-old imagination).

Like dragons, dinosaurs came in many shapes and sizes: the tank-like ankylosaur, the joust-ready triceratops, and the spike-tailed stegosaurus to name a few. But their reign over Planet Earth came to an end when ten-mile-wide meteor slammed into the Yucatan Peninsula and wiped them out 65 million years ago. Or so most scientists believe.

People didn't start unearthing dinosaur bones until the 19th century, long after dragon legends began flying about. So, the tales of dragons couldn't have been based on dinosaurs.

Could they?

What if a species of flying dinosaur had survived, in small numbers, long enough to share the earth with our distant ancestors, who passed stories of them down to their children and their children's children and their children's children's children? Alligators are holdovers from the same time period, so why not pterosaurs?

It's the kind of daydream that leads people on pilgrimages to the Scottish Highlands in hopes of catching a glimpse of the Loch Ness Monster. But there's nothing wrong with daydreams; they're the stuff of stories, and if those stories endure over time, the stuff of myth.

The language of myth has enthralled me almost as long as dragons and dinosaurs have. It may tell us little or nothing about our true history, but it says a lot about who we are and how things might have happened ... if *we* were writing the stories.

Writing stories is what I do, so writing one about my twin childhood fascinations with dragons and dinosaurs just made sense. If anything, I'm surprised it took me this long to put one down on paper.

What follows is my own fanciful notion (laced with some scientific tidbits and a healthy dose of magic) about the origins of dragons, or specifically, one very special dragon. The only one, in this tale. Her name is Tara, a transparent nod to the word pterosaur, which means "flying serpent." She's the hero of our story, and she's quite the exceptional dragon.

I'm sure Puff would approve.

1

Arrival

 ontrary to popular opinion, history doesn't run in a straight line. Time might. Perhaps. But history generally doesn't. Confusing the two is simple enough, but unraveling the tangled mess that results from that confusion is a good deal harder. Imagine cleaning up the desk of an absent-minded accountant who, despite his good intentions, got his credits confused with his debits and his receipts mixed up with his bills.

Once you do, you'll have a good idea what it might have been like to sit down at the desk of one E.O. Spinesetter, Esq., after he got up from his chair and departed for wherever he went after he was here. "Here" being nowhere in particular, but for the sake of convenience, we'll say it was in a forest not far from an ancient village called Camel's Lot, which was located either on the Thames or somewhere a long ways to the west, in Cornwall.

It goes without saying that there were not camels in England at the time in question (whenever that might have been, it was a long time ago), except for one, which had been brought to the region by an Arab trader whose ship lost its way and wrecked somewhere on the coast of England instead of winding up in Morocco, where it was headed.

At least, we think that's how it happened.

Morocco might have been called Mauritania at the time, or maybe Carthage. England might have been called Britannia, or Albion. But at this point, everything's foggier than the mists that envelope the Thames during the mistiest time of year, which is to say we might not have the foggiest notion what they were called in the tongues that were used by the people that lived there whenever-it-was. But we can guess.

Kingdoms came and went with alarming frequency in those days, their names forgotten before they could be placed on maps, which were even less accurate than the few historical records that survive. Those same old maps that often included crude drawings of dragons lurking at the corners of a pancake-flat world. The flat-earth idea was discredited long ago, but dragons? They're another matter entirely.

Dragons are common in literature. They were, you might say, as common as herrings — the red variety, that is. In point of fact, while alleged dragon sightings were as routine once upon a time as UFO sightings are today, dragons themselves were the opposite. There weren't a lot of them. To be precise, there was just one; hence, the title of our story.

But before we meet our one and only dragon, we must return for a visit to the desk of E.O. Spinesetter, Esq., an esteemed man of advanced years whose back was slightly hunched from all the time he'd spent bent over the papers on that desk. One might have guessed, from his name, that he was a physician. But, no, the spines he set were those of books, the first to have been bound in the modern fashion.

It is said he came up with the idea after becoming exasperated with scrolls that kept rolling up as he ate raspberry crumb cake. A notorious fussbudget, he was continually unrolling the scrolls he had completed to make revisions or improvements, and the messy confection kept coming apart on him, falling down the front of his tunic and onto the document, smudging the ink he'd set down a moment earlier.

We know all this with absolute certainty, because history is perfectly accurate in all cases. Or so we think.

E.O. Spinesetter's name has passed into obscurity largely because his heirs thought it sounded too much like that of a disreputable acquaintance of theirs named J.A. Bonecrusher, who did, in fact, crush bones for the king when taxes came past due. They adopted, instead, the more straightforward Bookbinder, with the result being that no one knows the esteemed Mister Spinesetter by that name today. His initials are more familiar, or, rather, what they stood for: Emrys and Osiris — Emrys being another name for Merlin, and Osiris being the name of an Egyptian god who conquered death.

If you think history and mythology don't get mixed and mingled like vanilla ice cream and sweet soda in a root beer float, you've got another thing coming. That's a good part of the appeal. And if you thought this would be a straightforward account of the Only Dragon Who Ever Lived, well, think again.

E.O. Spinesetter, Esq., was a wizard. He was not the first wizard who ever lived, nor was he necessarily the last. It's just that those who've come after him have been a little more discreet about letting folks know who they are, having learned from that fame isn't the healthiest condition for a learned man to cultivate. (Just ask Socrates where it got him.)

It's not that E.O. Spinesetter went galavanting about making a spectacle of himself, waving his arms frantically and raising his scepter in the air as though he were trying to conduct a symphony. (That was Moses.) He didn't wear purple robes adorned with stars and moons, but instead went about in his nightshirt, valuing comfort over style in nearly all circumstances. But myth had its way with him, as it does when embellishing on history, and the wizards who came after him had to live with the consequences of his fame — or infamy, depending on one's perspective.

E.O. was a recluse, a homebody and, like most learned men his age, a curmudgeon. He didn't care for the outside world, preferring to cultivate the internal workings of his own mind, even if it drove him a little stir crazy from time to time. One of the first things he had learned as a boy was that the outside world was an unforgiving place, populated by people who thought they knew more than they did, and who did things before they thought about them.

These fellow humans wound up fighting with one another endlessly for no particular reason, other than the fact that it suited them. E.O. had no use for such petty distractions, so he retreated to his own abode, a cozy cottage in the woods he had disguised to look like an oak tree so that he might not be disturbed. Except it didn't quite work out that way.

Disguises are all well and good for avoiding trouble, unless someone decides the thing you're disguised as is worth attacking. For the most part, an isolated cottage in the woods that looks like an large oak tree isn't likely to draw much notice, unless it happens to be struck by lightning. But unfortunately for our friend E.O., the woods in question served as a boundary between two warring kings, each of whom had laid a claim to the area after E.O. had established his. Before long, they had begun sending their men into the area from opposite sides, and it was only a matter of time before there were fireworks.

It was annoying enough having his peace and quiet interrupted by the clash of weapons and the sound of war cries, but then King Balathorn's men began clearing a path through the wood by clearing brush and hacking down trees. This sent poor E.O. into a panic, not merely because he feared the loss of his home, but because it contained a treasure trove of dutifully spine-set volumes on everything from zoology to alchemy (something E.O. never managed to master, but then again, neither did anybody else). He had collected so many volumes over the years that, if his oak tree were threatened, he could never possibly manage to move them all.

If he had been the Merlin of myth, he would have simply stepped outside his oak-home, raised his scepter to the sky, uttered a few dozen words in a language no one else could understand, and cleared the woods of the interlopers with a mighty wind. But E.O. Spinesetter had no such flair, or love of the dramatic, and even if he had, he wasn't nearly as adept at such things as subsequent legends might have us believe.

So instead, he merely created a new disguise that made it look as though there already was a path through the woods, whereupon Balathorn's forces plunged ahead ... directly into the invisible trees, cracking their heads on unseen branches and falling headlong over roots that "weren't there." It was a messy business, and E.O. had to keep himself from laughing at the men stumbling about, crashing into things and one another until they were so thoroughly disoriented that they wound up going back the way they'd come.

He had solved the problem for the time being, but E.O. knew the men would be back, and that their counterparts from Wyriven's kingdom on the opposite side would have to be fended off, as well. He knew he would need a more permanent solution to his problem.

Another man might have simply pulled up stakes and moved to a different wood in a different part of the country, far away from kings and their petty bickering. There was plenty of land as yet unclaimed by any humans, let alone self-declared "nobility," but E.O. could see by the rate of their procreation and their ability to adapt, that it wouldn't be long before more kingdoms would spring up and more woodlands would be cut down. Human beings would learn how to tame the land, if not how to care for it properly. (They were very good at learning, but mostly when it came to the wrong sorts of things.)

This was one reason E.O. was so stubborn. He was determined to only learn the *right* sorts of things. But it must be admitted that he had a less noble purpose: Like most men of a certain age, he liked things the way they were, and he wasn't about to let a bunch of second-rate, brass-plated hoodlums chase him out of his home in the name of some king whose authority he didn't recognize for some purpose that he considered nonsense.

All war was nonsense, in his book, but other humans

seemed as stubborn about waging it as he was about staying put, which presented him with his current problem. The two kings weren't going to give ground, and he wasn't about to, either. Which meant there would be conflict, and conflict was the very thing he was trying to avoid.

What to do? What to do?

He was pondering this very thing the morning after King Balathorn's forces went staggering back to their encampment, the answer quite literally fell right out of the sky. It announced its entrance with the crackling of branches overhead and landed with a thump just outside his oak-house. It, or, more precisely, she.

She was a winged creature, but unlike any bird he'd ever seen, and he had been around long enough that he was fairly certain he'd cataloged every specimen in this particular stretch of woodland. Shrikes, sparrows, larks, starlings, finches ... This was none of those. She was much larger — about as long as his forearm, but he could tell from the look of her that she was a juvenile. The strangest thing about her was that she was almost entirely bereft of feathers; her two wings were more like bat wings, but with the skin ridged in row upon row.

The creature was making odd, distinctly non-bird sounds. In fact, the sounds were more like a wheezing or grunting than any chirping. It almost sounded human.

She didn't have a beak the way a typical bird would have, which led him to conclude she was not a bird at all. What she was, he didn't know. But he knew she was young, and he knew she was resilient, because despite the force of her fall, her eyes were open and she was gazing up at him with a look he would have sworn held a spark of intelligence. Young intelligence, true, but intelligence nonetheless.

She blinked at him, narrowed her eyes, then widened them, as though she recognized something in him, as well.

"What's your name, little one?" he asked. "Who are you? *What* are you?"

She squeaked.

"Do you mind if I take a look inside your mouth?"

He knew she couldn't understand him, but he was, by nature, a polite person, all the more so because he lived alone and hadn't had as much occasion to grow impolite through the crude exchanges most humans had with one another. Woodland creatures were, by nature, more considerate of one another than humans, except (of course) when a predator was on the hunt. Then, being considerate went out the window. But at least most predators only took what they needed; they didn't keep killing and killing to acquire more land and more gold and more wine stains down the front of their fancy shirts.

The flying creature (who wasn't currently flying) didn't resist when he reached down and opened her mouth; the inside was lined with two sharp, parallel rows of teeth that looked like they would be quite formidable when she grew to adulthood.

How big might she get?

E.O. noted how much her mouth — which was shaped roughly like the wolf's on the outside, ending in something resembling a short beak — resembled the anatomy of a human's on the inside ... except for those obsidian-sharp teeth. The shape of the palate, the way her tongue could press up against it ... he wondered if, just perhaps, she would be capable of speech.

She spat his fingers out of her mouth and narrowed her eyes. Was she glaring at him?

Intelligent. She was definitely that, who and whatever she might be.

She was also hurt. One of her wings was moving, but she was keeping the other one very still, apparently on purpose.

"It hurts, doesn't it?" E.O. muttered. "You must have landed on it wrong."

He stretched forth his hand and touched the wing gently, but the creature recoiled.

He nodded knowingly.

Stay right there!" he told her, though it was clear she was still a bit dazed and unlikely to go anywhere. He rushed back inside and returned carrying a quilt his mother had made for him years earlier. Wrapping her in it, he brought her inside and laid her in a small wheelbarrow, a contraption he had invented himself but had no current use for. It was a makeshift solution, but it would have to do until he could figure out something else. He didn't expect she'd be with him for long; he'd see that her wing was healed and she was strong enough to fly, and then he'd send her on her way.

Fate, it so happened, had other plans.

STEPHEN H. PROVOST

2

Settling In

 ne should be careful about the questions one asks, even idly and even in the confines of one's own head. That's especially difficult for those of a scientific persuasion, E.O. Spinesetter being a prime example.

It was as if the universe had heard him ask himself, "How big might she get?" and had decided to answer him in the most hilarious and inconvenient way possible.

Over the course of the few weeks after her arrival, the

19

creature had grown from the size of E.O.'s forearm to the size of his ... well, of *him*, complete and whole. And she hadn't stopped growing yet. Much of that growth was in her wings, which consisted of a layer of skin stretched out from one incredibly long finger and attached to her body like twin sails. Her hind legs, by contrast, didn't seem to grow much at all. They were a little like tree stumps with pudgy feet and knobby toes. E.O. thought they were funny-looking, but he tried not to stare, because when he did, she always stared back at him — disapprovingly, he could have sworn.

Sometimes, she would waddle around on those legs, but more often she would go on all fours, stretching her wings out to the sides and in front of her, half-pulling herself along on the shorter fingers of her tiny hands, halfway between her body and wingtips. E.O. still didn't know exactly *what* she was. Nothing in the zoology texts he had accumulated over the years looked remotely like her. So, when he was done consulting them, he started experimenting with combinations of various animals, based on stories he'd heard in his travels. He had never seen any of these things himself, and until now had considered them flights of fancy from the imaginations of men with too much time on their hands. But he would have said the same of the creature now in his care, had he not seen her with his own eyes. So he looked back at the notes he had taken upon hearing these fantastical accounts, just in case Mother Nature was trying to play a trick on him.

He came upon an Egyptian merchant's account of a

beast called a gryphon with the body of a lion and the wings of an eagle, which he sketched out quickly on a leaf of parchment. But it looked nothing like the creature in his care, who glanced over her shoulder and cocked her head as if to say, "That's a terrible likeness."

Next, he found a description of something called a crocotta, which had come courtesy of a squire making his way back from a fierce battle on the steppes of the great

northern continent. The flustered young man had tripped over his own tongue relating the story of how his knight had been slain by a beast with the body of a stag, the neck of a lion and a hideous mouth ready to devour any it might come upon. But his guest looked nothing like that, either.

In Persia, he'd heard tales of the chamrosh, a winged dog, and, in Eygpt, of the famed phoenix. Like the phoenix, his guest had wings, but beyond that, there was little resemblance. At length, after combing through all his notes, he resigned himself to admitting that he had simply never come across the likes of her before.

She would, however, need a name, so he took to calling her Tara, after the most common sound she made — an insistent "te-RAAH!" — whenever she was hungry.

E.O. soon found that Tara had a peculiar diet. Whenever a fly would go buzzing past, she would open her mouth and snap at the air in a single quick motion and a fierce finality. Such was her natural aptitude for this mode of hunting that the unfortunate insects never managed to escape. Her prowess at snagging flies and gnats and even honeybees (which she swallowed without flinching, even as he worried she might have been stung) was hardly enough to sustain her rapid growth. She therefore took to hunting the mice that invaded his grain stores, much to his delight, as his beloved but aging gray-white tabby Argentus had proven far less adept than a cat should be at keeping them away.

One morning, to his dismay, Argentus went missing, and E.O. undertook a thorough search of his home in an attempt to find him. The usual coaxings with catnip and fish scraps failed to draw him out, and he began rummaging through cupboards, opening chests and crawling under tables (despite his arthritic knees), all the while finding no sign of him. It didn't help that Tara gobbled up the fish scraps he'd left out, and he scolded her for it. She looked wounded; he would have sworn she understood more than his tone of worry disguised as anger.

Was she worried, too? Or, perhaps, just guilty?

And was she guilty about *more than just the scraps?*

The thought occurred to E.O. before he agreed to entertain it, because he didn't *want* to entertain it. But there it was, and once it took hold in the back of his mind, there was no way to dislodge it. He was a man of reason, and all possibilities had to be considered, even if they were disturbing — sometimes, if one was to be honest, *especially* when they were disturbing. He didn't want to believe that Tara might have (gulp) *eaten* Argentus, but she was clearly an omnivore with a prodigious appetite, and poor Argentus had become so slothful in his dotage that his bulging belly might have seemed tempting, even under all that fur.

Could Tara ...?

Would Tara ...?

He looked at her out of the corner of his eye, shook his head, and said simply: "This fish is for Argentus. If you want some, I can get you some later."

He did a double-take. Had she nodded?

Impossible.

He turned and started making kissy noises with his lips and clicking sounds with his tongue. "Here, Argentus! Here, Kitty! I have your favorite treat right here waiting for you."

A moment later, a sleepy-eyed Argentus emerged from one of the many hidden nooks that are known to exist in the homes of aging wizards.

"Meow," he yawned.

"Meow." This time, it wasn't Argentus.

The cat's eyes widened. He was suddenly awake, and he scampered away on his fluffy paws faster than he should have been able to at his age.

E.O. spun around, his eyes wide as well, staring at the source of the sound.

It was Tara.

That was when E.O. discovered that Tara had the ability to mimic sounds, very much like a parrot. The idea seemed even more feasible now: If she could make those sounds, and if she was as intelligent as she seemed to be, then perhaps she was capable of truly communicating with him.

He began making it a habit of speaking to her directly. He presented simple, one-syllable words while showing her what they meant: bread, chair, stool, hat, door, book ... In each case, she immediately repeated the word back to him and, when he nodded toward the object, she did so, as well. The nodding came in handy when he tried a different exercise: asking her simple yes-or-no questions. She learned quickly to respond with a nod of her head when she agreed with his proposal (usually involving whether she wanted this or that kind of food), and a loud snort when she did not.

At the end of each day, he sat down at his desk by candlelight and made note of all she had done, and when he went back and read over it all, he was astonished to find that her achievement level matched that of human child. From the way she was growing, he guessed she wasn't much more than a toddler herself. But that was only a guess, based on how fast she was developing and how her appearance had changed, even in the short time she had been with him.

How much longer would that be? That was the question he kept asking himself. He was a solitary person by nature, and it felt odd to share his home with someone for such a length of time. Tara was different than Argentus; more like another person (no offense to his cat, whom he loved dearly) than a beast.

He poured himself a cup of tea, flavored it with some honey, and sat back to think.

He was worried. It had been nearly two moon cycles, and Tara's injured wing had healed quickly, but she had yet to even attempt to fly. She was so quick to learn things like language and his daily routine that it seemed strange she had yet to experiment with those wings of hers. Then something occurred to him: Although her wings were growing fast, perhaps they still hadn't grown enough to keep her aloft. Baby birds are always shy about leaving the nest, and every now and then, a mother will nudge a fledgling over the edge before it's ready. Looking back, he wondered if that hadn't happened to Tara. She had fallen from the sky like a meteorite, but when he had looked up toward where she'd come from, there'd been nothing unusual to see. Patches of blue sky dotted with strands of white cloud. Tree branches, undisturbed save for their movement in a gentle breeze.

Except, now that he thought about it, there hadn't been any breeze that day ... except in that single moment. And it hadn't come from the east or the south or the north or any other direction on the compass. It had come from overhead. He hadn't taken conscious note of that before. But the realization had lain dormant in some dark corner of his memory, waiting for him to notice its relevance.

The most likely conclusion: Tara had been dropped, accidentally or otherwise, by something with wings large enough to stir up the air down on the forest floor. Something, very possibly, just like Tara. Maybe this young creature didn't know what her wings were for — that she was *supposed* to fly. He shook his head; he didn't think so. She was too smart for that. Probably, she was just scared. She didn't know whether she *could* do it, and was afraid to try.

How could he possibly encourage her? He was afraid that, if he tried to push matters, he'd only make things worse by bringing back the memory of what had happened before. Now, though no choice of his own, *he* was the "mother bird" who would have to come to terms with how and when his baby would leave the nest.

It was in that moment that E.O. Spinesetter, Esq. realized that, even though he guarded his privacy enough to build his abode in the middle of a forest and make it invisible to any who passed that way; even though he found the company of others tedious and intrusive; even though he was an old curmudgeon set in his ways and jealous of his time; even with all that, he had grown so fond of Tara that a part of him didn't want her to leave.

"Harrumph," he said, under his breath. And then, "Oh, well."

He shrugged his shoulders and drifted off to sleep in

his chair, the half-cup of remaining honey tea growing cold on the table beside him as he began to snore.

STEPHEN H. PROVOST

3

Thievery

"low down! Slow down!" Long Dashi admonished the young man who had burst into the room of his secluded home in the bamboo forest. Only his trusted acolyte, Long Pengyou, knew where to find him. He had taken Pengyou in when the boy was brought to him as an infant, an orphan whose parents had died in the great conflict between two warring dynasties. The war had been so brutal that one-third of the population had perished, and it was because of this that Long Dashi had withdrawn into the bamboo forest.

Having no children of his own, Long Dashi had shared his own name with the child, and had named the boy Pengyou, which meant "friend" (for Long Dashi had no idea of how to be a father, but believed that friendship was the key to ending the wars that had plagued his mighty nation before the rise of the present, noble emperor).

"Tell me again what you are saying, Pengyou," he said.

Pengyou's dark hair tumbled into his eyes over a warm and sweaty brow. He had run a long distance from the village, where he had gone to trade some of Dashi's wares for pork and rice and noodles in the marketplace. Long Dashi and Long Pengyou never wanted for delicious fare at their table, for the goods Dashi sent to be traded were always in great demand. Because he was a wizard, like E.O. Spinesetter, he knew how to create tools for farmers seeking to bring in a bigger harvest more quickly, instruments that measured their yield for them and even ingenious games to occupy their youngest children.

Pengyou's chest rose and fell as he struggled to catch his breath.

"I am sorry, Master, I fear I have ..." his voice trailed off and he stared down at his feet.

"You fear you have what?" Dashi asked. "And you know there is no need to call me Master." Pengyou only called him "Master" when he had done something he thought would bring shame down upon him.

Dashi's voice was patient, not demanding. It was never his tone that struck fear into a man when he spoke, but the fact that it was Dashi who was speaking.

Pengyou raised his eyes tentatively and seemed to wince as he allowed them to meet Dashi's.

"The goods you meant to send with me to bargain with at the market ..."

"Yes?"

"Please, Master, forgive me, but I left them on the floor in the storehouse for safekeeping ..." his words came more quickly now "... and I took instead the other sack that I left near it, which looked the same to me because I was in a hurry, and ..."

"Other sack?"

"The one you gave me for safekeeping. The one that contained ..."

"Are you telling me ...?"

Pengyou's eyes fell back to the floor again, and he nodded slowly.

Dashi's eyes flashed, not in anger, but in fear. "It is not your fault," he said, his voice soothing as he stepped forward and placed his arm around the boy's shoulders. Pengyou had seen only a dozen years of life; perhaps Dashi had asked too much to ask of him. This had been an important task, and Dashi knew that one only gained wisdom on the back of true responsibility. He had known the risk, a risk that had now become fact.

"Where are the fire flowers now?" he asked, his tone unchanged. "Do you know who has them?"

Pengyou shook his head vigorously. "I had never seen them at the traders' market before. They were foreign, with fair skin, hair the color of sand, and beards on their chins that

31

were dark and bushy.

Dashi nodded. "Men from west of the world you know," he said solemnly. "But how could they have known you had the fire flowers and not the implements I had meant to send away with you?"

He stopped for a moment to think. It was, he felt sure, mere chance. Men from the west had been seen at the market before. They did not come often, but whenever they did, they quickly learned of Dashi's wonders and sought to trade for whatever Pengyou might have with him, knowing it would be useful.

If they understood it.

With any luck, these latest visitors would not know what they had or, if they discovered its nature, how to make use of it. But luck had not been on Dashi's side when Pengyou mistakenly picked out the wrong sack to take to market. Dashi did not trust luck, and less so fate, which seemed to side with the selfish and the greedy far too often to lend him any comfort.

"Did you see where they went?" he asked, but Pengyou shook his head.

"They vanished into the crowd. I only discovered that I had given them the fire flowers when I returned to the storehouse to check on them and found the implements you had given me for the market there instead."

"I see." Dashi's voice was flat. He wasn't disappointed so much as he was worried. It did no good to mourn the past when the future held far greater risks. "Then we must send a message to a friend of mine who lives in the world to the west. Many birds will be required to fly over many lands, and its delivery will be neither sure nor easy, but it *must* be attempted. Do you understand?"

Pengyou sensed the worry in Dashi's voice and nodded vigorously. "It will be done, Master," he said, "even if I have to fly there with my own two arms."

Dashi laughed heartily at this, and Pengyou managed a weak smile. If only they didn't need to rely on tiny birds and men who imagined they could fly.

STEPHEN H. PROVOST

4

Mission

"What am I?"

"That is the question, isn't it?" E.O. Spinesetter, Esq. chuckled as he sat across the table from Tara, who had grown so large that she had to keep her head down just to fit inside the largest room in the old wizard's small abode.

It had been six months since her arrival, and she was speaking, if not perfectly, easily enough to be understood and to understand, in turn, what her host was saying.

"You must know. You are the smartest man in the world."

E.O. chuckled again. "And how would you know that? You've never met any other men."

"I know you. That is all I need to know."

E.O. did not know any such thing himself. The more one knew, the more one realized how much there was to learn — and how very big the world was beyond the edge of his little forest. E.O. didn't travel anymore, but he had done so in his younger days and had made many friends who kept in touch, sending him messages by way of carrier pigeon and mutual acquaintances.

One such message had arrived just a day earlier. It had been sent by a certain wizard on the other side of the world in a place called Zhongguo that many believed was mere legend. E.O. knew differently, though. He had seen this magical land with his own eyes. Its forests were more vast than the whole of Britannia; there were great deserts, and broad stretches of frigid land to the northeast. It was a land of proud emperors, fierce warriors and creatures he might have  consigned to his list of legendary beasts had he not seen them for himself. Rotund black-and-white bears that were no bigger than a man's fist at birth but grew to be nearly a thousand times that size. Dogs that appeared to be part raccoon. Huge tigers with stripes like a zebra and leopards of similar coloring.

Men of great wisdom dwelt in this land, and one of them, named Long Dashi, had gained such great renown that his reputation had passed beyond the bounds of Zhongguo to the world beyond. He had studied the stars, it was said, and had learned how to make rain and call fire from the sky. This fire could be captured, he claimed, and launched skyward where it would explode and cascade down over the land below.

E.O. marveled at this, and it worried him, for he knew that if such a wonder should fall into the hands of the warring kings, they would certainly turn it against each other to cause great destruction. That is what Long Dashi had warned in his missive, which told of two westerners who had accidentally come into possession of what he called "fire flowers." This must have occurred some time ago, knowing the amount of ground that would need to be covered by any number of pigeons in relaying the information from Zhongguo to Britannia.

There was every possibility that the two men who had procured the fire flowers had arrived before Long's message, and although it was also possible that they had been bound for Gaul or Germania or Iberia, he was unwilling to take that chance. If they were typical merchants, they would want to sell their goods to the highest bidder, and both Balathorn and Wyriven had made it widely known that they were willing to deplete their substantial treasuries, each to defeat the other. If one could get his hands on the fire flowers before the other ...

E.O. Spinesetter knew he had to prevent that, because he knew it was only a matter of time before they invaded his forest again. Things had been quiet — too quiet — in the preceding months, and he sensed this meant each of the two kings was plotting some large assault against the other.

"What are you thinking about?" Tara asked him, and he realized that his gaze had drifted toward the ceiling, as it often did when he was lost in thought. She was perceptive, this one, but E.O. had no wish to reveal what he was thinking. Wizards are known for keeping things secret when necessary (and sometimes when not so necessary) for fear of unveiling wisdom that others are not yet ready to see. E.O.

did not think Tara was ready to see the reality of how men destroyed each other and the land in their quest for power, but he knew that if he failed to act, she might see it in any case.

He had to protect her, and he had to find out more about these fire flowers. Time was of the essence, and he knew he wouldn't have time to send word back to Long via carrier pigeon and wait for his response. He needed something more immediate. As he pondered how to get word quickly to Long and how to keep Tara from harm, he hit upon an idea of how he might accomplish both these things at once.

Tara's wings were strong enough to carry her the entire distance in a small fraction of the time it could be covered by pigeons. By sending her to Zhongguo, he could keep her out of harm's way and find out all he needed to counter an attack by the two kings. There was just one complication: Tara still had not tested those wings of hers in flight. She had been reluctant to even climb up to the lower limbs of the forest for fear that she might fall again, as she had on the day he first encountered her.

"Tara, there is something I must ask of you," he said. "And it will take great courage on your part, but it is of the utmost importance."

Tara sat up straighter and bumped her head on the ceiling, eliciting a pained squawk from her beaked maw. "I will do it," she declared when she had recovered.

"Splendid!" E.O. responded. "I must send you on a

journey to a faraway land, and you will have to fly to get there."

Tara's shoulders slumped and her head fell. "But," she said meekly, "I do not know how."

E.O. looked at her, his eyes serious and beseeching. "I cannot do this myself," he said, "but I *know* that *you* can. I have to get a message to an acquaintance of mine far away. If I do not, I fear that our home and, indeed, the entire forest might come to ruin. Please tell me you can do this. Much depends on you, my young friend."

"What if I fall and the message never reaches your friend?"

"Then you will have done your best, and you will have done more than anyone else can do. This task, I am afraid, can only be accomplished by someone of your ... wingspan."

Tara nodded solemnly. "Then I shall try. Perhaps your friend can tell me what I am."

"I know what you are," E.O. said. "You're the bravest person I know."

5

𝕱light

.O. tried to be patient. If he'd had his way, Tara would be airborne over the channel between Britannia and Gaul at this very moment, but he knew she wanted to take things slowly.

That proved to be difficult, however, from a practical standpoint. The way Tara's wings were designed, it was better for her to take off from a high place and find an updraft to glide along on, rather than flapping them furiously to gain altitude. There wasn't much room for flapping in a forest crowded with trees, in any case.

She tried climbing up to the lowest level of tree branches and launching herself from there, but there wasn't enough time to catch the wind — or enough wind to catch — before she landed on the ground again with a thud. When he suggested she climb higher, her entire body started to shiver in fear, and she clung desperately to the tree trunk, scared to even glance at the ground below her.

E.O. could see this wasn't going to work. If she tried taking off too close to the ground, she'd just fall, and if she started farther up, she would probably still fall — and might hurt herself in the process. He was sure the memory of how she'd landed on his doorstep was coming back to her each time she tried climbing one of those trees, and it was apparent that he'd have to try something different.

Tara was about to climb up again when E.O. beckoned her back down. "That's enough for this day," he said. "Tomorrow, we're going to try something different: We're going to have to leave the forest."

E.O. knew that if he could take Tara to the white cliffs facing toward Gaul across the channel, the winds would bear her aloft and carry her eastward. That would only happen, however, if he could persuade her to jump from a height far greater than any tree in the forest. And he had to get her there first, traveling over land through the heart of King Balathorn's

42

kingdom without anyone paying heed to the imposing creature at his side and sounding the alarm about a "monster" in their midst. She was too big to hide inside his wagon, so she would have to travel in the open. The best he could do was create a disguise that made her appear to be a very large horse — which required that she keep her now-massive wings tucked close to her side — and hope nobody noticed the clumsiness of her gait or how misshapen she was. It was fortunate that wizards are good at disguises.

Tara nodded in agreement when he shared his idea, but she didn't seem too enthusiastic about it, even though E.O. tried to instill confidence in her by tying the note to her leg that he'd written to Long Dashi. He suspected she was agreeing because, to her, anything was better than jumping out of trees and crashing again and again. He tried not to let on that he was even more worried than she was. She hadn't had to deal with any humans except for him, and she had no idea what cruelty they were capable of.

He did.

Was he asking too much of her? In his quest to keep her safe from the war he knew was coming, was he placing her in even greater danger? He didn't know. But something inside kept telling him not to turn back, even when they came upon a small party of King Balathorn's soldiers traveling directly toward them on the seabound road.

There was no use trying to avoid them; if they diverted their course once they'd been seen, it would only attract suspicion.

One of the soldiers rode out ahead of the other half-dozen in the party and came up to meet them. They weren't career soldiers, but rather, farmers and herdsmen pressed into service by the king. Still, they did their utmost to look suitably impressive in their maroon tunics, greaves and bronze breastplates (some of which didn't fit particularly well).

"Good day," the lead soldier said as they approached, introducing himself as Prefect Corax. He was a squat man of early middle age with a ploughman's muscles and a lazy right eye.

The soldiers all dismounted. "That's a ... sizable mount you have there," Corax said.

"Indeed," E.O. said. "A fine draft horse. Not so good for riding, but you make do with what you have."

Corax nodded. "I bit strange looking," he said, scratching his chin, "but ..."

Tara gave a snort of derision that sounded nothing like the kind of sound a horse would make.

Corax stepped back involuntarily, then recovered his wits and stepped forward. "He'll do ..."

"She," E.O. interrupted. "And do for *what*."

"We're confiscating him ... her for the war effort."

E.O. drew himself up to his full height, which was appreciably taller than the prefect (although, with his slight and spindly build, he still weighed significantly less). "You most certainly are not."

Corax laughed in a way that sounded like his namesake. ("Corax" in Latin meant "raven," but it could also be translated as "battering ram," and the prefect looked every bit that part as he stepped right up to E.O. Spinesetter, Esq., and puffed out his chest.) "King Balathorn has decreed that the property of whosever might cross his lands may lawfully be seized for use in the sacred war," he said flatly. The tedium in his voice made him sound like an actor reciting the same line from the same script for perhaps the hundredth time.

This was precisely what E.O. had been afraid of. As has been stated, he was not the sort of wizard who raised a staff over his head, uttered ominous curses and called down lightning from the sky. He was the sort of wizard who buried his nose in books and, although he did carry a staff, it was strictly for keeping himself properly balanced as he walked. There was not a lot he could do against a half-dozen soldiers bearing swords and spears, even if they were only a few months removed from shovels and pitchforks.

Corax sidestepped E.O. and reached up to take hold of

the makeshift bridle the wizard had designed to fit Tara's slightly less-than-horse-shaped head.

Tara had never been this close to any human being except for E.O. until now, and she didn't like it. Not at all. Very much like a horse, she reared up and shook loose the prefect's grip as though he had been a caterpillar clinging to the edge of a leaf.

The prefect tumbled backward onto his rear end and started scuttling backwards on all fours, his eyes wide as he stared upward. The other soldiers took a step back and drew their swords, watching as the "horse" in front of them unfurled a pair of gigantic wings. Tara flapped them with such force that that it blew the soldiers back two more steps.

But that wasn't far enough, because she charged forward at them, mouth open to reveal those two rows of razor-sharp teeth. She kept right on flapping her wings as the soldiers' hesitant retreat turned into a panicked withdrawal. Breaking ranks, they ran off in all directions, pursuing their spooked horses, which were likewise fleeing. A couple of them were so badly shaken that they dropped their swords, while the others gripped theirs all the tighter.

It was then that something happened that no one, least of all Tara, expected. Her short but powerful legs had managed to push her forward fast enough that the air billowed up beneath her powerful wings and separated her from the ground.

E.O. saw the stunned look in her eyes and thought it must have mirrored his own when a gust of wind curled itself up under the two giant flaps of skin and bore her upward as though her wings were sails on the open sea. Moments later, the look of surprise was replaced by an expression of wonderment.

"I'm flying!" Tara exclaimed, and E.O. answered her, "So you are!"

She tumbled and banked as the winds eased and kicked up again, learning to navigate them on the spot. She was a natural. Of course she was.

In the distance, E.O. could see that four of the soldiers had managed to retrieve their horses and were staring up into the sky at her. Emboldened by the distance between themselves and the "monster," they sheathed their swords (those who hadn't dropped them) and shouldered the bows that had been strapped to their mounts. E.O. could see they were taking aim at Tara; he couldn't tell at this distance whether they were in range or not, but he feared the worst.

"Go!" he shouted, but Tara hesitated and a volley of three arrows flew skyward toward her, one falling just short and the other two barely missing on either side.

"Go! Now!"

This time she did, flapping her wings as she caught a tailwind that sent her eastward faster than he could have imagined. Balathorn's men didn't even have time to nock another arrow by the time she was gone.

They looked back in the other direction, their eyes scanning the horizon in search of the old man who had brought that horrendous beast into their midst.

He was nowhere to be seen.

6

To Zhongguo

 ara flew as fast and as far as she could each day, and when she grew tired, she searched for a high mountaintop far away from any human dwellings. The behavior of King Balathorn's soldiers had told her all she needed to know about humans — at least those not named E.O. Spinesetter — and she had no need of further evidence concerning their character.

Even in avoiding human contact, however, she faced some challenges. The first was that she had to learn to find food for herself. No more of the hot tea, buttered biscuits with marmalade and salmon that she'd enjoyed on a regular basis in E.O.'s home. Now she had to fend for herself, and it occurred to her that she didn't even know what a creature like her she was *supposed* to eat or how to go about getting it.

By trial and error, she figured out quickly enough that she didn't like tree leaves, mushrooms or flower blossoms. When she flew over a wide river that seemed to stretch endlessly to the horizon, however, she had a revelation. Where the river was calm, she could see creatures swimming just below the surface, and the sight of them awakened something inside of her that said, "Food!" She swooped down low over the river, setting birds to flight and sending small animals skittering away in all directions as she dove for the water. Opening her mouth wide, she scooped up a large, unsuspecting fish and tossed her head back gleefully as it disappeared into her mouth. She rose quickly again, chewing on it eagerly as she ascended, and realized the taste was familiar — very much like the salmon E.O. had served back home. In a moment of realization, she understood that this *was* a salmon; though it was raw, it was still delicious.

From that time on, she stayed close enough to one of the many rivers as they crossed open land, but moved to a safe distance whenever a human settlement came into view. Once, she carelessly flew too close to a town and heard the sound of voices shouting up at her from below. Men came rushing out of their houses, screaming, some of them aiming longbows at her the way Balathorn's men had, but none was close enough to reach her. She banked south away from the village and flew low beyond a ridge of hills, moving safely out of sight again and returning to the rivercourse once she was safely beyond inhabited land.

The rivers here seemed to run roughly in the same direction as the sun's daily path, and she followed them toward its rising, which was the direction E.O. had sent her.

Still, she was no pigeon, which meant finding her destination was a far greater challenge than finding food. She had never been there before and didn't have the slightest clue about how she might find it, other than the vague directions E.O. gave her based on his own travels. By land. Many years earlier.

Occasionally, she would spot an expansive forest or a large body of water and think she was on the right track, but she couldn't be sure. The journey seemed as though it would never end, and there were many times Tara feared she might be so far off course that she would never find what E.O. called the bamboo forest.

Tara didn't know what bamboo was, although E.O. had done his best to describe it to her: a long, stiff stick that grew up out of the ground like grass but that was many times larger and had ringed ridges at intervals along its length. Not a thing like a regular forest.

Whether she was getting close or had even possibly passed it without knowing, she couldn't tell. She had never been farther than a short distance from home before now and could not have imagined how far the other side of the world might be: Even with her great wings to carry her, it was a very, very long way.

After a while, the towns grew scarcer and the trees shorter. She flew over a series of inland seas, taking many hours to cross each one, and afterward followed a line of mountains that rose higher than any others she had seen so far. E.O. had told her about these, so she was finally sure she was on the right path as she continued eastward.

Tara had been told to be on the lookout for three bright red flags at the edge of a village near the confluence of two rivers. This, E.O. had told her, was the village closest to the small estate of Long Dashi, within the bamboo forest only a short distance farther on.

Long Dashi was the one who had learned the secret of the fire flowers. It was he who had sent word to E.O. that some of them had been stolen by men from the western world, and it was he who feared they might wind up in the hands of men who would use them for ill.

Tara feared she might miss the three flags if she strayed off course or flew past them in the dark of night. And what if the villagers neglected to fly them because it was storming? She was beginning to despair that she might never find them when, one evening just past sunset, she saw them at the place where the waters of two rivers came together: three ripples of crimson flying in a strong wind against the darkening sky.

She flew onward a short distance and soon found herself over what seemed like a giant meadow of grass, with stalks that looked to be nearly as tall as she was.

E.O. had told her how to approach Long Dashi, who would not be expecting her and would likely be startled at her arrival. Wizards were famous for their composure, but even they had their limits, he said. She was to arrive as quietly as possible, fold her wings immediately and announce herself boldly as a messenger from E.O. Spinesetter, Esq., speaking in a different language than the one he had taught her to begin with. He had explained that not all humans shared the same tongue, and in the short time before she departed, he had hastened to teach her a few words in the language he said she would encounter.

Tara landed at a clearing in the bamboo, which grew so thick in places it was impossible to see more than a very short distance ahead. She had seen what looked like the wizard's home from the air, but the minute she landed among the strange emerald green stand, she was no longer entirely sure of which direction she should go. The maze of stalks looked just about the same in all directions, and she looked this way and that, then up at the sky to find her bearings by the stars.

I think it is that way, she said to herself, and started off. But she immediately found it impossible to follow E.O.'s instructions about staying quiet. She was simply too big to pass among the bamboo stalks without snapping some of them, and the cracking noise they made set birds that were roosting there to flight. There was more cracking, too, from a land creature of great size, and she thought she saw an orange-and-black striped line of fur ripple through the stalks off to her left. It must have known this place well, for it made far less noise than she did even though it seemed as large as any beast she had seen. She heard what sounded like a muffled roar, which convinced her to veer off slightly, away from it.

There were no more noises, apart from those made by her own passing, so she set her gaze back up to the sky and began following the stars again, unaware that the bamboo stalks were growing gradually thinner before suddenly parting altogether to reveal a small channel for conveying water ... which Tara didn't see, either. She tripped over it and was sent splashing and sprawling forward, face-first, with a startled yelp that sounded just a bit like the cry of a whooping crane.

She heard a shout in what sounded like the language E.O. had introduced to her, but she didn't recognize any of the words. The voice came from behind a dwelling across the clearing, and before she could regain her composure and clamber back to her feet, a human boy came rushing around the corner.

Then, he stopped in his tracks, eyes wide.

Tara hurriedly stood to her feet and spread her wings in what she intended as a gesture of friendship. The boy, though, must have interpreted it differently, because he shouted, "aaaaaaRAHHHH!" and threw both hands in the air, tripping over his own feet as he rushed into the dwelling. She was pretty sure "aaaaaaRAHHHH!" wasn't a word in *any* language, not in the proper sense.

Someone else must have been inside the dwelling, because a moment later she heard two voices speaking back and forth, one of them frantic and hurried, the other measured and calm.

After a moment, another figure emerged in the doorway and stepped out onto a wood-plank porch in front of the building. He was a man, much older than the boy, of average height and with graying wispy hair; the way he carried himself, moving with assurance and without haste, reminded him of E.O.'s bearing. He didn't seem frightened at the sight of her, but intrigued. Nonetheless, he remained at a safe distance; she could see that he was sizing up the situation.

The boy, who was peeking out from behind him just inside the doorway, clearly *was* frightened.

Tara straightened her back and raised herself up in a way that she had hoped would appear serious but, from the boy's reaction, might have seemed more fearsome than anything else. He hunkered down to half his height and tugged on the man's sleeve, trying to pull him back into the residence. The man, however, did not budge.

"Greetings from the western isle of Britannia," Tara announced formally, reciting the words E.O. had taught her.

The old man seemed surprised to hear her speak his language, or perhaps to hear her speak at all. Tara had noticed that not a single creature except for humans spoke audibly in anything other than grunts or barks or snarls or chirps. These were a form of language, E.O. had told her, but they were language based on tone and inflection alone, rather than on enunciation of specific syllables. Since she had yet to encounter another of her kind, she realized, it must seem odd for a human to hear anyone but another human use actual words.

She continued. "I bring you a message from your friend E.O. Spinesetter, Esq., in response to your own message. It is bound to my leg. Please remove it at once and read it carefully."

The old man cocked his head to one side, then chuckled and took a step forward.

The boy tugged at his sleeve once more in vain before letting go and stepping back inside behind the doorframe, his two eyes darting to the large winged creature, then to the old man and back again.

Tara stayed perfectly still as the man took another deliberate step forward. He pointed to his chest and said "Long Dashi."

Tara recognized that. It was the name of E.O.'s friend. She was in the right place.

Raising a wing and pointing a finger on one of her small hands toward her own chest, she said, "Tara."

"Tara," the man repeated, and took two more steps forward. "Welcome."

That was one of the words E.O. had taught her, along with the appropriate response. "Thank you," she said, bowing her head and closing her eyes. It was a gesture of trust and respect, which E.O. had also taught her.

Tara heard the boy gasp in the doorway, his two eyes fixed on her as the man strode slowly up to her and stretched forth his hand toward her leg. "May I?" he asked. She wasn't sure what the words meant, but the inflection told her it was a question, so she said, in his language, "Yes."

"Thank you," Long Dashi said, and reached forward to take the leather pouch that was fastened to her leg with a sturdy cord. Tara hoped that E.O. Spinesetter's message had remained safe inside during her journey. She had been able to avoid the storm clouds that occasionally drifted toward her as she flew, veering to one side or the other so as to protect it from the elements.

Loosening the pouch, Dashi removed it and untied the leather cord so he could reach inside and remove a single scroll. This he opened and read aloud. Tara couldn't understand it in his language, but she knew what he said because E.O. had read it to her before sending her on her way.

My dearest friend Dashi,

I received your message concerning the theft of the fire flowers and share your concern that they might end up in the wrong hands. War has broken out in these lands, and I fear I am in the middle of it, with one king's armies at the eastern edge of my forest and another king's forces to the west.

Either of these men would pay handsomely for what you say was stolen from you. I do not know what skill you used to create them, so I fear I could neither make them myself nor — as would be my true intent — neutralize them. I need your help to do so.

Please send instructions back with Tara so I may know how to proceed. Treat her your own kind hospitality, as if you were entertaining me in your home. Happenstance brought her to me, and I am hopeful that it is for a great purpose such as this. She is remarkable, as I am sure you will discover in short order upon meeting her.

Time is of the essence.

Your friend, E.O. Spinesetter, Esq.

Dashi frowned and shook his head, then looked up at

Tara. He pointed to the scroll and then to himself, shaking his head and spreading his arms wide. "I cannot," he said, and this she understood among some other words that she did not. "Cannot stop them. But come," he said, beckoning with his hand. "You" — he pointed to her, then wrapped his arms around himself and nodded — "are my guest."

STEPHEN H. PROVOST

7

𝕾𝖆𝖈𝖗𝖎𝖋𝖎𝖈𝖊

ara was grateful for Dashi's hospitality. He served her soybeans and cucumber (which she ate politely but didn't really care for), tofu (which tasted to her like mushrooms with less flavor) pork (which was tasty, if not so much as salmon) and tea (which reminded her of home, even if it wasn't quite so sweet as what E.O. brewed).

The boy gradually overcame his fear of her, which gave way to fascination as he ventured closer and closer. More than once, Dashi had to tell him to stop staring, as it was impolite, whereupon he would avert his eyes quickly and pretend not to keep looking out of the corners of them.

The boy's name, she learned, was Long Pengyou, and despite his initial fright and subsequent curiosity, she could tell she was just as kind as the old man.

They ate their meals in the storehouse, which is where Tara also slept because she was too large to fit inside Dashi's main residence. (She wondered if she would be able to fit in her own home back in Britannia when she was returned, as she had barely been able to do so at her departure and was still growing at a prodigious rate.)

Everything about her stay at Dashi's estate was pleasant, but she was restless at first. She knew E.O. had wanted her to return at once, and it seemed at first that Dashi was delaying her, keeping her there when she was needed back home.

Before long, however, she understood why he wanted her to tarry.

He wanted to teach her.

First, he taught her to better understand his language. He left most of this to the boy, who he said was already a "loyal friend" and would make a "good teacher" once he learned "patience" and "understanding." These were some of the first words she learned.

More importantly, though, he had been considering how to help E.O. solve his problem, and he had come up with a plan, but he needed Tara's help to carry it out.

"I am not even certain I should ask this of you," he said. "But I can think of no other way. Perhaps the fire flowers have not found their way to Britannia, and into the hands of men who would use them for ill. But even if this is so, do you think your home is safe?"

Tara dipped her beaked mouth into the huge bowl of hot tea before her, then raised her head again. "I do not know."

"Did you not tell me that men of war had already invaded your forest?"

She nodded slowly.

"If they come with fire flowers, they may destroy your home in days or weeks. If they come without them, it may take months, yet still, it will happen. With fire flowers, thousands will die on both sides, and this we cannot allow. But even without them, hundreds will perish because of what is in men's hearts. I believe the fire flowers may hold the key to stopping them."

"How can I help?" she asked, and he told her of his plan, which seemed strange at first, but made more and more sense the more he explained it.

"Are you willing to do this?"

"Yes."

"I must warn you, I am not even sure whether it is safe to take this first step. I have never done this before. It might work, but it might not; and if it doesn't, the reaction it causes ... well, it might kill you."

His expression was so serious one might have called it stern if not for the well of compassion behind his eyes.

"I understand."

"And if it does work, it will put you in even greater

danger. You will be hated and treated like the worst of demons."

Tara hesitated only a moment. "Men hunt me already. They do not like me because they do not know me. They do not *want* to know me — neither who nor what I am. I don't even know what I am myself."

Dashi shook his head slowly. "This will be a thousand times worse," he said. "People run from you now because they misunderstand you. They fire arrows at you and are relieved when you fly away from them. But if you do this, they will seek you out. You will be hunted to the ends of the earth by men intent on your destruction. Can you accept this?"

"Yes," she said, a tinge of sadness in her voice. "If it will get them to spare E.O. and our home in the forest."

The old man bit his lower lip. "You know," he said slowly, "that you will never be able to return there. It will not be safe for you. To ensure that E.O. and his forest home are safe, you will have to stay as far away from there as possible."

"For how long?"

"For the rest of your life, I'm afraid. If you survive. Those who wish to destroy you will follow you to the forest, and they will not spare E.O. Spinesetter, either."

Tara bowed her head low. She hadn't considered the possibility that she would never see her home again, but the way Dashi had explained it, she realized why this must be so.

"If I do this, the forest will be safe?"

"For a time, yes. I cannot guarantee anything with

certainty. Wizards cannot see the future. We only know enough to forecast what might happen in many possible futures. The more knowledge one has, the better one is at predicting."

"You have more knowledge than anyone I have ever met, except for E.O. But even he did not know how to create the fire flowers, and you know this ... so I will trust you," Tara said.

"Had I known what peril the fire flowers would create," Dashi said, "I might not have brought them into being. I suppose I was not very good at predicting this particular future." He shook his head. "No use second-guessing bad first guesses," he said. "It is decided. Save the rest of your tea for now. I believe you may need it to get rid of the aftertaste."

8

Ramphy

ara returned to Britannia the way she had come, staying close to the rivers except where humans had built settlements alongside them, as they often did. This time, she flew away from the sunrise, westward beside the giant mountains that bordered Zhongguo to the south. From there, she would travel across the steppes and great inland seas at the center of the expansive land mass beneath her, and the grasses of these steppes would give way to scattered forests and more human settlements.

Very few lived in the high mountains, though: no one save a few solitary souls who had withdrawn from the busyness below to pursue a life of contemplation. Not unlike E.O. and Dashi, she thought.

Tara had survived the first stage of Dashi's experiment, although it had given her an even worse stomachache than a batch of E.O.'s burnt scones. Fire flowers weren't meant to be eaten, any more than those charred scones had been. But they hadn't been meant as weapons, either. Long Dashi had created them as a way to celebrate life, he'd told her, as a colorful tribute to all that was good in the world, a display meant to reflect the joy of being alive, not a means of destroying it.

Dashi's fears that the fire flowers might cause far worse than a bad case of indigestion had failed to materialize. She'd been queasy for a good twelve hours, but that had been the extent of it. What remained to be seen, however, is whether they would do what Dashi intended. It was entirely possible that they would simply pass through her digestive tract and the whole enterprise would be for naught. But Dashi said he had never seen any other creature with an anatomy as — what had he called it? — as *sophisticated* as hers. From what he could see while examining her, he thought it possible that the elements in the fire flowers might be absorbed into the lining of her stomach and enable her to do something no other creature had ever done.

There was no better place to test this than a patch of thick ice on the jagged slope in front of her. Inhaling deeply, she reared her head, held her breath to the count of three and exhaled as hard as she could from the depths of her lungs, pushing up with her diaphragm and making a sound like air escaping from a bellows.

Nothing else happened, though.

She tried again, with the same result, then a third time, and a fourth. Maybe Dashi had been wrong about this. A part of her hoped he was. It meant she could go home again to E.O. and everything could be the way it was before, at least for a little while. But if Balathorn or Wyriven did get their hands on the fire flowers, they might use them to burn down the forest. What if E.O. was asleep when it happened? What of all the other woodland creatures who might lose their homes or even their lives?

She had to keep trying. Maybe she was doing something wrong. The queasiness she had felt after eating the fire flower had gone away, but she still felt the remnants of a chafing, burning feeling at the pit of her stomach. Perhaps if she sought to pull that feeling upward, at the same time she was exhaling, it might create the desired result.

She almost stopped the moment she started, because it felt as though she might be sick, but that feeling subsided as she began to exhale and noticed what seemed like very hot air rising from deep within her. Excited, she exhaled as strongly as she could and watched with amazement as a stream of fire came shooting out of her open mouth, and hit the ice on the mountainside. She was able to keep it up for nearly a whole minute (her lung capacity was considerable), until she heard a rumble and a loud crunching sound. Water was dripping off the ice now, and a huge crack was forming directly in front of her, where the stream of fire had made contact.

There was a roaring noise as the lower part of the ice

broke free from the upper portion, as well as from the mountain itself, and slid downward in a cloud of billowy snow-like crystals.

"It worked!" she said aloud.

"So it did. Congratulations. That's a neat trick. I've never seen anyone do anything like that."

Tara wheeled around in midair at the sound of the voice, which had spoken in neither the tongue of E.O. Spinesetter nor that of Long Dashi. Still, she understood it instinctively, as though it were her native tongue.

There in the sky, flying close by, was a creature that looked very much like her. It nodded its head toward her, and she nodded in response. "What ... who are you?" she said, taken aback.

"I'm Ramphy," he said cheerily. "I'm your kin."

"I've never seen anybody like me before," Tara answered.

"There aren't very many of us. Our kind came here many generations ago because there weren't any humans here to hunt us. I think they've forgotten about us. No one climbs this high into the mountains except for a few men in long robes who think we're messengers from another realm because we can speak their language." He laughed. "I haven't seen you here before, though."

"I'm not from here."

He didn't ask her where she *was* from, and she didn't volunteer it. He looked a lot like her, but with a few slight differences: He had a longer tail and a head that looked more like a snake she'd seen slithering around Dashi's gardens than it did like hers.

"How do you do that?" he asked.

"Do what?"

"What you just did — blow fire at the mountain."

"Oh. A friend of mine taught me how to do it."

"Can you teach me?"

"No, you have to have ... certain traits."

"That's not very nice," Ramphy said, wheeling in the air above her and then dropping down to look her in the eye. "I'm every bit as good as you are!"

"I didn't mean it like that." Tara was feeling defensive, but she didn't want to. Ramphy was the first of her kind she'd run into, and she wanted to know more about him. "What kind of creature are you?" she asked, changing the subject. "I mean, what do you call yourself."

"I told you. Ramphy. We're all called Ramphy. Names aren't really important. It's what's underneath them that

71

matters. We recognize each other by sight — by our markings. We don't even usually talk, but I tried to signal you before and you didn't pick up on it, so I decided to try the old language." He puffed out his chest as his wings buffeted the air, allowing him to hover in just about the same position as he spoke. "Most of us don't talk at all anymore. The language is dying. The only reason I know it is that my sire wants to keep it alive. I don't think he'll be able to, though. There aren't enough of us left who use it."

"I'm sorry," Tara said.

"Don't be. It's a new age now, the age of men. We don't belong here anymore, not even in this place. We won't be here very much longer."

"Where will you go?"

"I don't know. We just won't be here. My sire doesn't even know whether it's a different place or something else, like a dream. He says the ancient ones knew, but his generation has forgotten, like mine is forgetting the old tongue. He says maybe we don't go anywhere, but maybe we will just not be."

"That's sad," Tara said. "I don't believe that."

"I don't either." Ramphy dove down underneath her, came back up behind and tapped her on the shoulder with a bony wing finger. "Miss me?"

Tara laughed. "Don't *do* that!"

Ramphy laughed too. His eyes sparkled merrily from a gold and green and orange face. "You should stay here. We can keep the old language alive, the two of us, and dream a new dream together. Maybe our age doesn't have to end just yet."

Tara thought about it. She knew that if she went through with what she'd promised Dashi, she wouldn't have a home to go back to. But this ... *this* could be her home — a real home with others of her kind. Maybe this is where her own parents had come from; maybe she should have been here all along.

She looked around and noticed that others like Ramphy were soaring through the skies, passing between mountaintops, diving and swimming in the eddies of chill wind that whipped through the high peaks. They all looked like Ramphy, except with slightly different coloring; they were similar to her, but not the same.

"I am not from here," she said.

"Perhaps not," said Ramphy, "but it still could be your home. You are welcome here."

"Thank you." Tara nodded. "But I have a home. And even if I never see it again, I must protect it from the humans who are attacking it."

"How?" Ramphy asked, then realization dawned. "Ah," he said, "with your fire!"

"Yes."

"I still wish you would stay. I like you" He bared his teeth in what she guessed was a smile, although it would have looked more menacing than friendly if not for the sparkle in his eye.

"I like you, too," said Tara. "But I must go quickly. My friends are depending on me, and it is a long journey from this place to my homeland. Maybe I will return, if I can, someday and visit you here longer."

Ramphy's eyes fell. "If we are still here," he said. "If our age has not ended."

"Time will finish the stories our hearts cannot know," she said wistfully. It was something she'd heard E.O. tell her once, and she didn't know if it was true, but she hoped it was.

"Farewell, then, friend," he said.

"Farewell," said Tara, and she noticed that the other Ramphys flying nearby had formed a circle in the air. She somehow knew that this was a sign of good wishes and safe journeys ahead.

Wasting no more time, she turned in midair and made off westward toward the setting sun. Only when she had traveled a good distance did she realize she had never told Ramphy her name.

What was it he had said? "Names aren't really important. It's what's underneath them that matters."

That makes good sense, she thought, and made a note to remember it so she could pass it along to E.O.

Then she remembered: She would probably never see him again.

9

Elyrian

he knocking startled him and woke him out of a deep sleep, the kind that comes upon you when you're older and you sleep more soundly during a warm and lazy afternoon than you do once the sun has set.

E.O. Spinesetter sat up in his chair and rubbed his eyes, knocking his glasses from the end of his nose, where he had set them before he nodded off during the third section of *Botany, Biology and Zoology from the Beginning of Time to the Modern Age*. (Like bound books, eyeglasses were one of his inventions, an idea he perfected long before it was rediscovered in the Middle Ages).

He'd been rereading it for the third time, trying to see if he had missed some reference to Tara's kind in what wizards considered the definitive work on the history of life. E.O. had known the author, a wizard named Lucretius Falderol who was extremely well read, but who had grown irritated when E.O. asked him how he knew what happened millions and millions of years ago.

"I've studied it," he'd said dismissively. "I've read. I *know* things!"

"But how do you know them and where have you read them?" E.O. had pressed him.

"Because I *know*. I've *read*. Weren't you listening, man? In all the places where one learns and reads these things. In the most respected books by the most respected wizards who came before us. Are you accusing me of *making this up*?"

E.O. hadn't wanted to press him any further, seeing that Lucretius Falderol was growing increasingly agitated and that he, E.O. Spinesetter, Esq., was no closer to an answer than he had been when he'd first asked the question.

He had to admit that, in consulting Falderol's book, he was doing the same thing that Falderol himself had done: trusting that those who had come before him had set forth an accurate account of things they had never seen for themselves, just because someone else had said it was so.

When clothes were handed down from generation to generation, they became tattered and frayed and soiled and, eventually, looked nothing like they had when they were new. Stories were much the same way; by the time they reached the modern age, they resembled their original form only superficially, if at all.

E.O. knew this, but what other choice did he have? He couldn't very well talk to the people who had seen these things with their own eyes, could he? They had long ago departed this world.

The knock came again, and he jumped, this time knocking the book out of his lap and onto the floor.

The knocking was, most assuredly, not being made by a woodpecker or wryneck. It was a human hand at the front door. The disturbing aspect of this was that no one knew he lived in this part of the forest. Even if someone knew to look, he had disguised his home so well that no one should have known it was there. Wizards were very good at disguises, and only another wizard should have been able to see through this one.

He paused. Perhaps it was just someone passing by, testing to see if the tree was hollow.

It came again.

E.O. Spinesetter sat very still, hoping that whoever it was would go away. If Wyriven or Balathorn had managed to procure the services of a wizard, that would not be a good thing. No, not at all.

He waited, holding his breath without realizing it, and exhaled when the knock came again. Whoever was out there was very persistent. This knock was followed immediately by a voice. A woman's voice: "I know you're in there, Emrys," it said. "I am not a servant of the men you fear. My name is

Elyrian, and I have an important message for you. I will not simply go away, so you might as well open up. It will save me a night sleeping in the forest and you the same night worrying about what I might want."

Elyrian. E.O. did not recognize the name, but he sensed that she was not going away.

"Very well, very well," he muttered. Still not entirely awake, he raised himself off his favorite chair and made his way to the door.

Grudgingly, he opened it and was met with the sight of a woman he didn't recognize but who seemed oddly familiar. She wore a purple shawl trimmed in gold, with a hood raised up to frame a porcelain-smooth, milky-white face. Strands of silvery hair peeked out from underneath her hood and trickled down over a youthful countenance, but her eyes belied that youth: They were grey and distant, like storm clouds rolling in from some lost horizon.

"Good day, Emrys," she said, smiling only so much that her lips turned up slightly at the corners of her mouth.

"Good day," he answered warily. "To what do I owe the pleasure?"

The woman who called herself Elyrian ignored his question and looked past him onto the floor, where *Botany, Biology and Zoology from the Beginning of Time to the Modern Age* was still lying. She raised an eyebrow. "A little light reading?" she said. The question was playful, but her tone was mirthless.

"I was trying to ..."

"Figure something out. Yes. You wizards are famous for your inquisitive minds."

"*You* wizards?" he smiled a slight smile of his own, incredulous. "I trust you're one as well, or I doubt you would have found me."

"Not exactly," she said, but didn't elaborate. "What was it you hoped to find in that book?" She was still standing in the doorway. "If you'll invite me in, I'd be glad to help you with your inquiry."

E.O. shuffled back quickly a couple of steps and bowed slightly. "Yes, yes," he said. "Forgive my lack of manners. Please do step inside, and I'll brew us some tea."

Elyrian stepped through the doorway but raised a hand to decline the tea. "I have no need of refreshment," she said. "Just your attention."

A slight scowl flitted across E.O.'s face before he banished it as his guest swept past him and bent down to pick up the book on the floor.

"This," she said, "is rubbish."

"Rubbish?"

"You said it yourself. Things passed down from generation to generation — after a time, they outlive their usefulness. The more recent entries in this volume are of some limited value, I grant, but the older passages are nothing but fantasy."

The scowl returned and stayed this time. "You've been eavesdropping," E.O. said. "What do you hope to gain by ..."

"Eavesdropping? No. I'm sorry that's what you think of me, but I couldn't have possibly been eavesdropping when you didn't say any of that aloud, now, could I?"

E.O. pursed his lips. She was right. He'd just been *thinking* that; he hadn't said it aloud. But then how did she know ... especially since she claimed not to be a wizard?

"Don't concern yourself," she said, patting his arm in a gesture of consolation that seemed more perfunctory than warm. "I am not offended. I merely meant to say that you were right: History books get less accurate the further they stray from the original events. What's needed is not a means of looking back at what was, but of looking forward with hindsight."

Looking forward with hindsight? What kind of doubletalk was this?

She sat down in his chair, holding the book in her hands as he remained standing there in front of her. "Wizards are good at some things, but somewhat obtuse in other matters," she said matter-of-factly. "You're very good at finding information on the outside, but you're not nearly as willing to listen to what's on the inside."

Before he could ask her what she meant, she went on.

"Another thing wizards are good at is predicting things. Have you ever wondered why that is?"

He stood up a little taller. If this woman was testing him somehow, he was determined not to make a fool of himself. "As you said, we gather information, and from that information, we discern patterns. We simply follow those patterns to their logical conclusion."

She smiled a genuine smile this time, one of true amusement. "That's very much what I would have expected you to say. It was the subject of a discussion you once had with Long Dashi, on your visit to Zhongguo many years ago, was it not?"

"Why, yes, but how ...?"

Argentus hopped down from atop a cupboard, where he'd been silently observing them, and slinked up to Elyrian, lowering his head to be stroked.

"He's taken right to you," E.O. remarked. "I'm

surprised. He doesn't see many strangers, and whenever he does, he usually stays in hiding."

"Surprised?"

"Why, yes. As I told you, he doesn't usually ..."

"You mean '*hasn't* usually.' That's in the past. What do you think he will do in the future? I mean, right now. What do you think he will do next?"

E.O. shrugged slightly and frowned as he pulled up another chair and sat in front of her. "It's late afternoon, so I suppose he'll go over to his food bowl and check to see if I've remembered to put some scraps there for him."

Elyrian shook her head and ... did she really roll her eyes? "That's what he usually does," she said. "I'm not asking you that. I'm asking you what you think he *will* do. Consider what he's done in the past, of course, but see how the situation has changed and then look *inside yourself* to see what *you* think he will do *now!*"

Before E.O. could answer her, Argentus jumped up into his lap and started purring.

"I was going to say that," he muttered, irritated and sure that she wouldn't believe him. But he was wrong.

"I know you were. Because I know how to predict things. You need to get better at it by trusting yourself."

She pointed to the book on the floor with one hand while she stroked Argentus with the other. He was purring. "That book there," she says. "Do you know what it is? Just a bunch of flawed information about what supposedly happened in the past — a lot of which really didn't."

"Yes."

"Well, what if you had a book that gave you information about what will happen in the future? And what if it was entirely accurate?"

E.O. chuckled. "I would have the answers I was looking for."

His guest bowed her head toward him. "And so, you do. Inside yourself. All of our potential, everything we can possibly ever be, was there before the dawn of time. All we have to do is know how to access it, and we can know what will happen beyond a whisper of a doubt, because we know how to make it happen. We have the outline of a perfect history book inside us from the beginning; all we have to do is write it, and once that's done, reading it is child's play. *That's how the wizards of old predicted what was to come. That's the skill you must recover to gain the answers that you seek.*"

"But how ...?"

"Read the history you write from the beginning, not what someone else has written seventh-hand."

She stood, and Argentus jumped down. He went running for his food bowl.

Reaching into a bag he hadn't noticed she was carrying, Elyrian withdrew a pristine book with a cover in light-brown leather that looked as if it had never been opened. The binding was immaculate, E.O. noticed, precisely matching his own high standards.

"I'm afraid that's all the help I can give you," she said, "and I'm also afraid I must be going."

"Let me show you to the door then," E.O. said, but before he could take a step in that direction, his guest had vanished. Just vanished, like that. He scratched his head and wondered: If she could do *that*, why had she bothered knocking in the first place?

Walking back over to his chair, he sat down again and opened the book she had given him. There, in his own handwriting, was the answer he had been looking for:

The world will pass through seven ages, and these are as follows.

The Age of Fire, before man or beast will walk the earth, when rivers of flame burst forth from inside the world to make and mold it.

The Age of Water, in which creatures smaller than a human eye might see (though no humans will yet walk the earth in that age), will inhabit the waters that envelope the earth.

The Age of Earth, in which the land will rise up from the seas and the creatures of the seas shall follow, growing in size as they emerge from the depths beneath the waves and hoist themselves onto the newformed earth.

The Age of the Jungle — of vines and ferns and great, soaring plants of all shapes and sizes. These shall flourish and provide the creatures of the land with much nourishment, so that they may grow and flourish as well.

The Age of Giants. On the earth, they shall be ten times larger than an elephant, with long necks and strong armor and sharp teeth. In the sea and air will be seen fantastic serpents that swim the seas and fly through the heavens on wings more majestic than any ever seen.

The Age of Ice, when the seas shall recede and the land shall freeze at the top and the bottom of the world. The great beasts shall perish, and new creatures shall emerge.

The Age of Man, an age of great enlightenment, but also of war and of strife.

Each of these epochs shall share some moments, one with the next, when creatures out of time may yet dwell in hidden places, venturing forth for but a moment, before vanishing forever into the mists of yesterday.

E.O. marveled at what he read. How could he have written this before it happened? How could he have known it *would* happen before he himself was even born? Elyrian had given him the book of which she had spoken, the book she said was inside himself. Somehow, she had conjured it out of thin air and showed it to him, for his own eyes to see.

And because of it, he had the answer to his questions about Tara: She was a survivor from the Age of Giants and beyond the Age of Ice, a creature "out of time" who had emerged from some hidden place to be seen in this, the Age of Man. He finally had the answer to the question she had asked him. He would have to tell her all about it when she returned.

And perhaps now he had a way to keep the war away

from their forest, even if she never reached Zhongguo and returned without speaking to Long Dashi. All he had to do was consult this book to find the answers. They were there; he was sure of it now.

But all this thinking and all this excitement were making him drowsy again. He felt his eyelids start to grow heavy, as he lay the book down on his lap and felt his spectacles slip down to the tip of his nose.

When he awoke, he felt refreshed again. Argentus was purring on the arm of his chair, and the book was still in his lap. Excitedly, he picked it up and gazed at the title on the cover: *Botany, Biology and Zoology from the Beginning of Time to the Modern Age* by Lucretius Falderol.

The real history had been inside him all along.

10

Overthrown

yriven sat on his throne and stared at the bedraggled specimen before him. Thrones in those days weren't the majestic display pieces they would become many centuries into the future. Wyriven's was little more than a wooden chair on a slightly raised pedestal. Not that this looked in the least bit out of place in a throne room that was little more than a glorified barn, and given that it was occupied by a man who was by no means imposing.

Wyriven was a spindly, short and bow-legged man in his mid-twenties who had risen to power after his older brother died in battle. He had stayed there more by cunning and deceit than by any prowess he had shown on the battlefield — which was none; he always made sure to stay well behind the front lines and let his soldiers do the fighting for him.

But if Wyriven was hardly physically impressive, the man before him was even less so. He looked as though he might have been, at one time, but in his present state he appeared gaunt and nearly emaciated. His clothes were torn and filthy, and his stringy, matted brown hair blended together with a long, wiry beard that drifted halfway down his chest.

It looked as though he'd been halfway around the world and back.

In fact, he had been.

"Who are you and what business have you before the throne?" Wyriven asked as his eyes wandered to one side. His tone betrayed extreme boredom; he had little patience for granting audiences to his subjects, and only did so if his advisors deemed it essential.

The man bowed low before him and looked as though he might fall down before straightening himself back up again.

"Sire, I am Aelfric of Westerbridge. I bring you a prize so wondrous, so potent that I guarantee it will enable you to defeat your enemy Balathorn once and for all.

Wyriven brought his eyes front and center. He was still bored, but a little less so. "And what, pray tell, is this prize you speak of?"

"A device that, in a single instant, gives off blinding light and smoke and fire, and at the same moment releases such power that it can drive a line of soldiers back on their heels, slaying the foremost among them."

Wyriven drummed his fingers on the arm of his throne. He was unimpressed. "Really," he said flatly. "I don't believe you. ... Guard!"

A helmed man in uniform took a step forward, but the bearded man raised his voice quickly in protest. "Wait, Sire! I can prove it! If you give me a chance, I can show you. I have one of the devices here with me."

Wyriven signaled the guard to stop with a lazy, backhanded wave. "Very well," he said, certain that the man was making the whole thing up. "Proceed."

The man named Aelfric opened a large cloth sack and produced a small, dark object with a bit of cloth sticking out of it, placing it on the floor in front of him. He then pulled out two pieces of flint and, bending down, struck them together near the cloth, which quickly caught fire.

"I'm supposed to defeat an army with *this*?" Wyriven said, but the last word was barely out of his mouth when the visitor rose and kicked the object toward him sending it rolling directly beneath his throne.

"What ...?"

There was a tremendous explosion, followed by a pinwheel of golden sparks and a stream of flame that shot straight up and engulfed Wyriven and the throne together.

The king began to scream, but his voice was drowned out almost immediately by a series of explosions that accompanied a shower of sparkling lights in a spectrum of bright colors.

The guard and three others went running as half the room burst into flames. None of them bothered trying to save Wyriven, whose reign had been established on the shallow sort of loyalty that comes from instilling fear, not the kind a ruler builds by being a true protector.

Allegiances shift quickly and easily under such circumstances, and they did so here, as well. Aelfric of Westerbridge had brought his own men with him to Wyriven's capital — men no more loyal than the king's but  who had seen what the fire flowers could do and whose fidelity had been purchased by the promise of riches to be won in conquest.

These men, who had been lying secretly in wait, rushed to Aelfric's side when they saw the flames rising from Wyriven's throne room. Wyriven's loyalists throughout the city either panicked and ran or joined them, unwilling to fight for a now-dead leader they had served only out of fear.

But Aelfric, despite his drawn and haggard appearance, was no mere opportunist. He and his partner, a fellow mercenary named Fal Borgain, had journeyed to the far east in search of fortune and had spent months there, learning all they could about their methods of warcraft, listening to whispers of those who held power and those who sought it.

When some of those whispers told them of a wizard who, it was said, could forge fire with his hands and unleash it with the force of a hurricane, Aelfric had scarcely believed it. But he had known better than to discount such stories without investigating them, and his inquiries had led him to a young boy in a remote village.

Fal Borgain had become that boy's shadow, following him, silent and unseen, for nearly a fortnight. He had seen what the boy had hidden in the storehouse and, by a stroke of good fortune, had brought to the market for sale one day. On that day, he and Aelfric had arranged to be there so they could relieve him of his merchandise. All without threats or arm-twisting ... or any of the more extreme measures they had been prepared to undertake in the service of their ambitions.

It had been so easy. Just as it had been easy for Aelfric to plunge a knife into Fal Borgain's chest as he slept and shove his lifeless body off the edge of a mountain pass two miles high. He had sent messages ahead to his network of mercenaries in Britannia, telling them to be ready for his return as he hatched his plot to overthrow Wyriven and take control of his kingdom.

Now that plot had come to fruition, but it was only the first stage in his plan. His next step would not be to consult with his military advisors, as one might have expected, but to seek out a wizard who could produce more of the fire flowers; he only had a few in his possession, and he had used one already to kill Wyriven. He would need more for what he had planned: a full-scale assault on Balathorn's kingdom that would allow him to consolidate power over southern Britannia.

Even before he had traveled east, he had heard whispers of such a wizard, a man who was said to live in the woodlands at the kingdom's border, although no one had succeeded in finding out exactly where. But Aelfric was, if nothing else, resourceful, and he was convinced that he would be able to ferret out the man's location and persuade him to help him achieve his goals.

He would lose no time in getting started. At once, he set about choosing scouts to send into the woodland in search of this wizard, but before he could give them instructions, the answer came to him.

In the form of a woman.

11

Compelled

.O. Spinesetter wasn't napping when the knock came at his door this time, but he did jump out of his seat, nonetheless. He wasn't expecting a return visit from Elyrian — certainly not this soon.

He stood up, tugging at the edges of his ruffled tunic and making a vain attempt to smooth his wrinkled trousers as he strode toward the door. He still had a vague impulse to look presentable, even though he had long ago forgotten exactly how to go about it.

E.O. nearly stumbled over Argentus, who was running frantic figure-eights between his legs. This was unusual, and he would usually have asked himself why the ice-blue-eyed tabby was so unsettled; but he was distracted and a little unsettled himself.

He should have paid more attention.

When he pulled open the door, the wizard was met not by the image of Elyrian, but by the faces of a half-dozen men in ragged uniforms armed with swords, clubs and spears. At their head was a gaunt man with a long beard and deep-set eyes that looked at once focused and highly volatile.

He did not recognize him.

"What is the meaning of ...?"

"This," the man in the front said, "is your chance to serve your king."

"I have no king," E.O. Spinesetter declared, drawing himself up to his full height.

"You do now, and you had best kneel before him, dog, if you want to keep that head of yours."

Another of the men raised a particularly sharp and hefty blade to illustrate the gaunt man's point.

E.O. did not kneel, so a burly man with a long black beard stepped forward, placed two thick hands on the wizard's shoulders and shoved him roughly to the floor.

E.O. looked up at him. "Who do you think you are?"

A thin smile spread across the gaunt man's face. "Aelfric, king of Britannia, slayer of Wyriven ... and your king. And I am here to command your service to the throne."

"I never recognized Wyriven's right to rule these woodlands, and I don't recognize yours, either. I don't even recognize *you*. How do I know you're not just some highwayman masquerading as a king?"

Aelfric scowled. "Not that I need to prove myself to you, but I trust this will suffice to persuade you." He held out his hand, and E.O. saw he wore Wyriven's signet ring. "Wyriven was a fool. He became complacent. Men of power are always vulnerable to those who walk among them, who study them, who learn their weaknesses and who know how to exploit them."

There was a degree of relish in his tone that E.O. found unsettling. He changed the subject.

"How did you find me?" Not only had E.O. disguised his home well, he had been diligent about erasing any tracks he made when he went out to gather berries or take a stroll in the woods.

"A woman visited you here a short time earlier, did she not?"

E.O. said nothing.

"She came to me afterward and told me of your meeting."

The wizard tried to stand up, only to be held down by the big man's rough hands. "She told you where to find me? What did you do to her?"

"Nothing," Aelfric said evenly. "She was very forthcoming, although she didn't actually tell me *where* to find you, but *how*. She said I should go back to the beginning and trust my instincts. Then she gave me a book with instructions on how to proceed. Oddly, it seemed to be in my own handwriting, but it was the first I'd seen of it."

E.O.'s eyes narrowed. That sounded like Elyrian, all right. But why would she help this man — a kingslayer by his own account — after having helped *him*, E.O. Spinesetter, Esq., solve the mystery of Tara?

"What did you do to this woman after she brought you her news?" E.O. asked.

Aelfric cocked his head and shrugged slightly. "I thought about killing her, but then I decided she'd be more useful to me as an advisor. Unfortunately, she disappeared before I could extend my 'offer of hospitality.'"

"Hrummph."

"I trust you will not be so ... ungrateful."

The man who had pushed him to his knees hauled him back to his feet and grabbed hold of one arm, while one of his cohorts took rough hold of the other. Together, they shoved him out the door, which they didn't bother to close behind them as they pushed him away from his home and toward what he knew would be a future in captivity.

• • •

Cats know things.

Dogs are very good at sounding alarms and making sure the entire world *is aware* that they know things. But cats just know things — often a good deal more of things — and don't really care whether anyone else does or not.

Most of the time.

In this particular case, however, the cat named Argentus found himself wishing he had been born a dog. He had known, for example, that there were soldiers outside E.O. Spinesetter's home (his own home, as well), and had tried to warn him that this was the case. But when cats run like furry whirlwinds between a human's legs, they're dismissed as being playful or silly. It just doesn't have the gravitas of a dog barking incessantly at the door until every woodland creature within half a mile is wide awake.

Humans — even wizards like E.O. Spinesetter, who are supposed to be more attuned to such things — are uncommonly oblivious when it comes to a cat's style of communication,  usually chalking everything up to "I'm hungry" or "pet me" or "leave me alone." That's not to say such things aren't near the top of a cat's vocabulary, but they're by no means the only things that concern your average feline. And Argentus was not average, not by any means.

For instance, he knew immediately what he would have to do once the men took E.O. away. He didn't know how, exactly, he was going to accomplish it, but he did know that it was imperative that he do so. Cats are, you see, much more successful in communicating with other animals than they are with humans. This is probably owing to the fact that cats are, by their nature, predators, and as such are good at getting other animals to pay attention to them. (Humans, being predators of a slightly more sophisticated sort, at some point became so full of their own self-importance that they entirely forgot how to listen.)

The men who were leading E.O. Spinesetter away didn't notice the silver-white blur that flew out the open door behind them, scampered up a nearby tree and began dashing from branch to branch above the forest. Humans not only don't listen to cats, they often don't notice them, in part because felines know how to move quietly and in part because most humans just don't care until a dead mouse shows up on their doorstep. The cat's purpose, to the humans' way of thinking, is to be of service to them.

Cats, of course, have other ideas. Humans, they're convinced, would be lost without them — and there is a good deal of truth to that proposition.

Argentus was determined to prove just how much.

12

𝔅luff

.O. Spinesetter, Esq., missed his afternoon cups of tea. He missed his books and the musty smell that escaped from between their pages when he opened them for the first time in many years, reacquainting himself with the wisdom of old friends. He missed the serenade of the nightingale and the woodlark, and he missed Argentus jumping into his lap, circling around once or twice, and curling up with a contented purr.

But more than anything, he missed his freedom. He had never liked cities, with their strident voices and stifling smells, even though cities in those days were a far cry from what they would one day become. Peace and quiet were his solace, but there was none of that to be found here. The sounds and smells of the city seeped in through the only window in his new abode: a cube of a room about ten feet long by eight feet wide, furnished only with a single table and chair. His bed was a heap of straw on an earthen floor.

He had been told he would be given whatever he might need to accomplish his task: replicate a device he had been given that Aelfric said was capable of exploding and causing an inferno simply by lighting an attached piece of string on fire. The device he was given as an example to follow was not equipped with the necessary fuse to ignite it

(his captor did not, after all, want him using it to escape), which made his task all the more difficult.

He had never seen anything like the device, but he knew immediately what it was: one of the fire flowers that Long Dashi had warned him about; Aelfric had no doubt used them to seize the throne but had no way of replicating them, so he had pressed E.O. into service in the hope that the wizard could help him do so.

Had Tara returned from Zhongguo in time, he might have learned from Dashi how to deal with these devices, but he had no idea what had become of Tara. Had she even reached her destination? Had she become lost or wounded somewhere along the way?

He had no way of knowing.

And he had no way of knowing, either, what he was

supposed to do with one of these fire flowers. That was a problem, because Aelfric had made it plain that any failure on his part would be construed as treason (even though he was not, in his own mind, a citizen of the newly named Aelfricland) and punishable by death.

Worse still, if he did succeed in his task, he would create the kind of weapon that would make Aelfric capable of destroying not only his own beloved woodland, but laying waste to all of Britannia and the lands beyond. That was the very thing he had been trying to prevent by sending Tara on her mission; he could not, under any circumstance, allow that to happen.

The biggest mystery in all this was the role of Elyrian. Why would she help him, then turn on him so viciously? Who was she and what was her motive in all this? She seemed to have disappeared after showing up suddenly on Aelfric's doorstep, just as she had done after visiting him. He felt like a piece on a gameboard being shifted around at the whim of a player.

As he was thinking these things, the door swung open and Aelfric strode in, flanked by a pair of guards, hands on the hilts of their swords.

"I trust you are making good progress, sir wizard," Aelfric said, smiling through half-clenched teeth.

"I can't very well make progress if you don't allow me to test my hypotheses, now can I?" E.O. rejoined.

"And I can't very well allow you to blow a hole in the

side of my building and go waltzing out of here. You're a wizard. So, do your wizarding!"

He turned abruptly and left, the two guards following and slamming the door behind them. He heard a wooden bar slammed down into place outside. E.O. found it galling that people who weren't wizards expected those who were to simply snap their fingers and make things happen. It didn't work like that, of course, but people were so scared of things they didn't understand that they made them out to be far more impressive than they actually were.

In some respects, this could be convenient: If people were afraid of you, they were less likely to bother you, and E.O. did not like being bothered. But when they wanted something from you, they thought you could fashion a pair of wings and fly to the moon or conjure up a cure for winter fever at a moment's notice. Then, when you couldn't, they accused you of holding out on them and got even more angry at you than they had been when they were afraid of you.

That was it!

Maybe if he made them afraid of him ...

"Guard!" he shouted.

"What is it?" came the thoroughly uninterested voice from the other side of the door.

"Tell your king I've figured it out."

E.O. heard a shuffling sound of the guard getting slowly to his feet.

"Be quick about it, man. I doubt he wants to be kept

waiting."

The shuffling sound became more hurried, then gradually faded away into the distance.

A few minutes later, the door opened again and Aelfric entered with his two bodyguards

"You've succeeded?" he said eagerly, rubbing his hands together. "Let's have it, then!"

"Oh, you'll have it, all right, sire ... unless you do exactly as I say."

The usurper frowned. "I'm the one giving the orders. Now tell me ..."

E.O. Spinesetter shook his head decisively and cut the man off. "You will free me to return to my home. You will not follow me, you will issue a decree forbidding anyone from ever setting foot in that part of the woodland on pain of death, and you will erase any record of your having come that way."

The king snickered. "Or?"

"Or I will use this device to blow us all to the next life right here and right now. I'm an old man. What will it cost me? A few years? It will cost you" — he paused for dramatic effect — "everything."

The king crossed his arms. "You can't," he said with purposeful decisiveness, but failing to disguise the hint of doubt in his voice. "I've seen how the devices work. You need a candlewick to make it work."

"Quite so, quite so," E.O. said, "for an ordinary mortal.

But you sought out the services of a wizard, and that's exactly what you've gotten. I have the capacity to make this device function, here and now, should I wish to do so. I'd rather not, but if you leave me no choice. ..."

"You're bluffing." Again, the king's tone was meant to convey certainty, but it was even clearer now from the slight quaver underlying it that the seed of doubt E.O. had planted was taking root. "If you had such power, why did you let us bring you here? Why go through all that trouble?"

"Someone once told me that — how did he put it? — 'men of power are vulnerable to those who walk among them, who study them, who learn their weaknesses and who know how to exploit them.' What better way than to learn a king's weaknesses than to visit his city?"

E.O. was aware he was pushing his luck, but the only way to make this arrogant king believe him was to behave even more arrogantly himself. If he betrayed even the slightest hint that he was trying to hedge his bets, Aelfric would call his bluff and, most likely, kill him then and there.

One of the guards took a step forward, but E.O. thrust the device menacingly above his head and fixed Aelfric with an intense, cockeyed stare that said, "I dare you."

"Wait," Aelfric said, and the guard backed away. "I will grant your conditions. I have others who can figure this out. I will grant you sanctuary within the woodlands, but only there." He turned to the guards. "Do as he has requested. Escort him to the city gates and see that he leaves. Do not follow him, and speak to no one of what has transpired. If you ever see this man outside the woods again" — he turned back toward E.O. — "kill him."

• • •

Aelfric returned to the makeshift throne room he had set up in a tent outside the old one he'd burned down, then called his chief minister, a former mercenary like himself named Ystaig, to him.

"How many of those fire flowers do we have left in our possession?" he asked.

"A handful," he said. "But none of the other men you charged with the task is any closer to replicating them than before."

"Perhaps that doesn't matter," Aelfric mused. "What's inside them?"

"A yellow crystal," Ystaig said. "It's quite common, actually."

"Where?"

"In the Bath springs, for one thing, where the infirm and elderly take their ease."

"I want you to take a group of men there at once and bring back as much of that crystal as you can carry. Take as many wagons as you need. When you've got it, take it to the woodlands and spread it in a direct line from this side of the forest to the other. Oh, and be sure the line runs past that wizard's treehouse." A thin smile spread across his lips.

"And once this is in place?"

"We will ignite the crystal, and it will burn a path straight through the woods for our soldiers to march on Balathorn's lands. We will conquer them, and I will have my revenge on that troublesome wizard in a single stroke."

Ystaig smiled, mirroring his master's grin.

"Now off with you and be quick about it," Aelfric said. "Balathorn will never know what hit him."

13

Return

ara was tired. She had flown a long way as fast as she could; all that exercise had made her wings more powerful than ever, but it had also exhausted her. Still, there was only a little ways left to go. She saw the strait that separated Britannia from the mainland stretching out before her, the whitecaps rising up and dancing in the sunlight of a speckled-cloud sky.

She knew her woodland home lay not far beyond.

She also knew she couldn't return there. Her mission was elsewhere, and a perilous one it was — not only for her, but for anyone or anything that might get in her way.

As she flew farther on, the mists began to roll in, as they were wont to do across the River Tamesas, and she felt the cool wetness dance across her face. It was refreshing at first, but then, after a time, there was another feeling — a constricting of her lungs and a burning in her eyes.

She banked downward through the clouds, which turned from gray mist to billowy black swirls as she moved onward. She was no longer flying through fog, but through smoke, rising from the ground below her. To her dismay, that ground was covered with trees, and she realized she was already over her woodland home.

It was burning.

Red and yellow flames leapt from treetop to treetop, borne by sparks that ignited them one after another in a straight line of fire pierced the heart of the woodland like a blazing sword.

Tara followed it for a time, fearful that E.O. Spinesetter's home might lie directly in its path. But the smoke was so thick here she could no longer see clearly; blinking away the burning embers that rose to claw at her eyes, she caught an updraft and rose higher, but the smoke ascended with her, veiling her eyesight and filling up her lungs. She flapped her wings violently to repel it, whirling in the air, but it was everywhere.

No longer sure which direction she was going, Tara banked sharply and flew in a direct line, trying desperately to escape the smoke before her breath failed her and hoping that she hadn't become so disoriented that she was diving straight toward the ground.

After a short time, the smoke gave way once more to grey mist, and the coolness of it was a welcome relief as she breathed it in. Then the mist cleared somewhat, along with her vision, giving way to scattered white clouds standing watch over an emerald green landscape of meadows and rolling hills. Had she gone all the way through the smoke or back the way she'd come? The sun's position told her she'd doubled back, and her mind began racing to figure out how she might get to E.O.'s home. She had promised Long Dashi she wouldn't go back there, but things had changed. She couldn't simply abandon E.O. if he was caught inside that inferno.

Before she could think any further, though, something shot past her head just a few feet away. Glancing down, she saw a group of men on horseback directly beneath her, aiming up at her with arrows nocked to bowstrings.

Another arrow shot past her, and still another, closer this time. She flapped her massive wings to climb higher, but found herself caught in a sudden downdraft that held her in place, all but motionless against the half-clouded sky. If anything, the wind was pushing her down, closer to the men beneath her. Her mind flashed to the time when she had

109

fallen from the sky to land on E.O.'s doorstep, and the panic she had felt then returned in a flood. Suddenly, she was in a near free-fall, the earth rising up to meet her, her eyes wide and her muscles seemingly paralyzed.

Another bolt released from one of the archers below whizzed up at her through the air and bit into her left wing, shredding a portion of the skin there and leaving it to flap in the wind. Not enough to affect her *ability* to fly, but enough to get her attention and remind her of the need to do so.

She winced in pain and spread both wings out wide, banking sharply just a few feet above the ground and finding the updraft that had deserted her moments earlier. Blood dripped from her wounded wing, and the pain was searing hot. Fear gave way to fury, and she turned midair, flapping her wings and facing down at the men below who were nocking yet more arrows to fire at her.

The rage built up within her, not only at what they had done to her, but at the dawning realization that these men might also be responsible for setting the fire that threatened E.O.'s woodland home. Almost before she knew what she was doing, she reared back and then thrust her neck forward like a slingshot, exhaling molten-hot fire in a powerful stream toward the men below her. The fire itself eclipsed her view of what happened next, but when it ceased and she looked again, she saw the charred remains of seven armored men and their steeds on the ground below, barely recognizable except for the outline of their bodies in the grass. A single horse bearing a rider was galloping in a frenzy away from the scene, toward a town on the horizon.

Tara knew she would have to go in the opposite direction, even if it meant going back toward the smoke from the woodland inferno. It was not safe for her here.

• • •

Aldeberin Caskill, ranger in King Balathorn's outland patrol, rode through the gates of the capital city and brought his horse to a stop in front of The Stag's Horn, an inn and public drinking house just inside the city walls.

The horse nearly collapsed as Caskill climbed down and staggered inside, demanding a flagon of ale in a hoarse and shaky voice. His face was whiter even than the usual shade for men in that cloud-covered land; part of his uniform  was singed, and half his beard looked like it had been ... burned off.

"What happened to you, man?" the innkeeper asked, clapping him on the back and presenting him with an ample mug.

Caskill coughed. "The forest's afire!" he gasped. "Got to ... get word to the king."

The innkeeper could tell the man was not himself. He knew Aldeberin Caskill, and the man was neither a coward nor easily shaken. But shaken he clearly was. Whether from fear or exhaustion or some combination of the two, the ruffian who had once bragged about besting a bear in single combat had been transformed into a quivering shell of a man.

He wheezed and spat, then raised the tankard to his mouth and drained it in a single swallow.

"Who did this?" the innkeeper asked as others began to gather, curious themselves about what had happened to the man.

"Not who," Caskill said, pounding the tankard on the wooden longtable as a bit of his assertiveness returned, thanks to the ale.

The innkeeper dutifully refilled the mug.

"Not who," he repeated. "What!"

"What, then? Don't keep us in suspense, man. Spill it!"

"It was bigger than a horse — two horses! With wings like a bat but huge! It flew in the air and rained fire down on us from its nose and mouth. Killed all the others. I was the only one who got out."

"Gods, man! Talk sense!" the innkeeper half laughed, half chastised. But the look on his face hinted that he didn't entirely disbelieve his guest.

"You didn't see it!" Caskill protested. "I did."

He drained the tankard again, and the innkeeper filled it without waiting for any coin. The others were buying more rounds of their own as they listened, so the story was payment enough.

"You saw an eagle!" one of them exclaimed.

"Or a bat."

"Look at him drink!" one of them exclaimed. "He was probably drinking before he saw it! Maybe it was a sparrow."

"Or a finch."

They all laughed heartily. But Aldeberin Caskill stood and rammed his fist into the table. He didn't wince at the impact. Yes, this was the same Aldeberin Caskill who had bested the bear, all right. He was getting his wits back, but he wasn't changing his story.

"I. Know. What. I. Saw," he growled. "It wasn't no drink. I don't drink before I go on patrol, and them who know me can tell you. I don't know what it was. A ... a ... fire serpent."

There were murmurs around the table. One man, who had arrived recently from Rome, spoke in Latin: "draconem." Others, only partly understanding, repeated it as "dracon."

One of them laughed heartily. "A dragon? Ha! Never heard of it!" he snorted.

Aldeberin Caskill picked up his tankard and threw its contents in the man's face. It dripped from his forehead down into his beard as Caskill stomped out, his resolve now fully restored.

"I have to tell the king."

14

𝕭est 𝕷aid 𝕻lans

he smoke was thinning as Tara flew back toward the forest. That was the good news. The bad news was what it meant: The fire had run its course. Below her, only a few spots of flame danced amid blackened tree trunks and charred undergrowth, exposed for the first time in years now that the forest canopy had been burned away.

Tendrils of smoke rose from some of the trees that still stood, most of them devoid of leaves, looking like ghosts of winter frozen in their tracks against an ash-gray landscape.

Tara recognized none of it. She had never seen the

115

forest from the air before, and even if she had, it would have been unrecognizable to her now. She searched, her eyes desperate, for any sign of E.O.'s tree-home, but found none. All she saw was soot and ash and smoldering embers.

She must have circled the woodland a dozen times before fatigue set in and she took flight westward, continuing in that direction until she happened upon a cave.

There she found refuge.

Tara was hungry. And thirsty. A doe wandered past the cave's entrance, her eyes flitting this way and that, out toward the meadow, scanning the area for predators, then in toward the blackness of the cave, where she caught an unfamiliar scent that caused her muscles to tense. The wind shifted a moment later, and it was gone, so she settled in to graze on some long grass that grew near the cavemouth.

Tara could have called up the fire from inside her and turned that deer into a feast. She thought about it for a moment; she *was* hungry. But the idea of food sent her thoughts back to the tea and biscuits E.O. used to serve, and by the time those thoughts were done wandering, the doe had wandered away.

Tara had no way of even knowing whether E.O. was
still alive. The entire purpose of her long flight to Zhongguo
had been to save E.O. and his woodland home, yet this had
been thwarted because she hadn't made it back in time.
Ashamed, she slunk off deeper into the cave, not wanting
anyone to see her. Maybe she would just stay here. Men hated
her anyway; they were always shooting arrows at her, and
now they probably thought she was the one who had set the
woods on fire.

Long Dashi had told her this would be the price of
succeeding in her mission, but that mission had been a
failure, and she was paying the price even so. None of it
seemed fair. It was pitch black this deep in the cavern, and
that seemed somehow fitting. She just wanted to sleep, and it
made no difference to her if she ever woke again. The world
to which she would awake was darker even than this cave,
and without E.O. to share it with, she saw no reason to
believe that the darkness might be challenged.

Drained, she lay down on the cold stone floor of the
cavern. Water dripped from above into a pool nearby in the
black.

Drip.

Drip-drip.

Pause.

Drip.

Something, a spider perhaps, skittered over her wing
and was gone.

Tara sighed and put her head down on the earth and felt something move. She heard a faint sound like the tinkling of a dissonant bell, but she was too tired to worry about what it might be. Before her eyes had been closed for a minute, she was asleep.

• • •

The scout rushed into Aelfric's tent, breathless, and bent to one knee hastily, lowering his head.

"My lord, forgive me, but ... there is ... an emissary ..."

"Get up, idiot, and slow down."

The man brushed himself off and stood, facing his sovereign.

"My lord," he began again. "An emissary is here to see you from Balathorn."

Aelfric raised an eyebrow. "From Balathorn, you say? What business does he have?"

Before the man could answer, a tall soldier in chain mail and leather stepped into the tent. He did not bow, instead acknowledging Aelfric with a quick nod of the head.

"Who are you?" Aelfric asked curtly. "State your purpose."

"I bring news from the east," he said. "Our land has been attacked by a beast the likes of which we have not seen. It rides the heavens on wings the size of a thousand eagles and rains fire down on us from the sky. So destructive is this creature that it laid waste to the entire woodland between our two kingdoms. King Balathorn has sent me here to seek a truce that we might combat this demon together. He awaits your response."

Aelfric's eyes widened slightly, and he swallowed. This was, indeed, an interesting turn of events. Balathorn, evidently, had no idea it was Aelfric's forces who had set the woods ablaze and had decided, out of some superstitious fancy, to blame an imaginary beast sent down from the heavens.

So much the better. Aelfric had been preparing to send an invasion force through the charred woodland to attack Balathorn's realm. Now, a better option had presented itself.

"Tell your king I accept his offer of a truce. We will dispatch support forces at once," Aelfric said. "We will bring supplies and armed men ready to help you defend your land. Such a threat to one realm is a threat to us all. We will prepare our company to depart within the day."

The man nodded curtly again. "I offer thanks in Balathorn's name," he said. "I shall inform him to expect the arrival of your contingent forthwith. We will, of course, provide an armed escort when it reaches our border."

"Of course," Aelfric said through thin lips that concealed an inward smile. He remembered Homer's story of how the Greeks had infiltrated Troy and taken the city. His men would treat Balathorn's kingdom to a similar fate, and they wouldn't even need a wooden horse to do it.

15

𝕭eginning

.O. Spinesetter, Esq. stood gazing at the remains of his home. He hadn't trusted Aelfric to keep his word and, so, when the usurper's men had left him at the edge of the woods, he hadn't returned directly home, as they had expected.

It had been a painful decision. He had worried about Argentus, but the old cat was still surprisingly light on his feet; and he was nothing if not resourceful. E.O. felt confident the feline would find his way out.

Still, he had considered returning because he had so badly wished to safeguard the thousands of books he had stored in his tree home. Studying those books, and writing many of them himself, had been his life's work, but now they were all lost to the flames. He had meant to make copies of them, but every time he had thought to do so, a new idea had demanded to be written down instead. Besides, where would he have stored them, that they wouldn't have been burned up, too?

As he stood there looking at the charred stump in front of him, shaking his head slowly back and forth like a sorrowful pendulum, he knew they'd all been lost. His history books. His science notebooks. His recipe collection. *Maps of the Known World. The Care and Feeding of Finicky Cats. Biology and Zoology from the Beginning of Time to the Modern Age.*

He stopped himself as that title came to his mind and he remembered Elyrian's words to him: "We have the outline of a perfect history book inside us from the beginning; all we have to do is write it."

All those books he had written had come from inside him. He would merely have to start over. At the ... beginning. What the woman had told him all made sense, in an odd, topsy-turvy sort of way. But what didn't make sense is her betrayal. Thanks to her, his life's work lay in ashes. He would have to start all over again, from the ... beginning.

"You'll no longer be able to rely on what you've accomplished: what you've read and what you've written. You'll have to rely on yourself again. On that which is inside you. That's what created all those things in the first place. That's where your power lies."

He didn't know whether it was his own voice or the woman's that he heard inside his head.

• • •

Tara's eyes flashed open.

"You'll have to rely on yourself again. On that which is inside you." The voice wasn't E.O.'s — not exactly — it sounded like that of a woman, but it *also* sounded like it had come from him. Had she just been dreaming, or was E.O. still alive, somewhere, communicating with her?

The voice faded along with her sleep, and she lifted her head in the darkness. There was that tinkling sound again. There was something underneath her; she could feel it. It was slick but not slimy, and it was cold. She couldn't see it, though, and had no idea what it was.

The movement, she decided was in response to her own stirring; whatever it was, it didn't seem to be alive.

She thought no more about it.

The water was still coming down off the ceiling, splashing into that unseen pool a short distance away.

Drip.

Drip-drip.

Pause.

Drip-drip-drip.

Pause.

Drip.

Drip.

Then came another sound, very faint, of something stirring in the cave. It was a hunter. She could tell because it moved in stealth, as if sizing up its prey, preparing to strike.

Her muscles tensed, and she remained perfectly still. She was as big as any animal she'd seen, but this cave was bigger than she was, and she had no idea whether some unseen, bigger-than-she-was creature lay lurking within, waiting to strike.

If the creature was large, it moved with great finesse. It was nimble and all but noiseless, using the dark to its advantage. She only heard it intermittently, gliding across the stone floor in a slight scuffling sound, then pausing, as if to confuse her, before sounding again briefly from a different direction ... but closer, always closer.

Impatient, Tara tilted her head back and released a glowing fireball toward the roof of the cave, illuminating a forest of stalactites that hung down, tapering into uneven points like crooked javelins.

The flame caused whatever had been stalking her to jump — she heard it distinctly this time — and in the sudden brilliance, the creature cast a massive shadow against the far wall. It was the shadow of a giant cat, teeth bared and back arched. E.O. had read to Tara from his books about the ancient Smilodon, the saber-toothed cat of yore that had disappeared when the ice sheets stretched across the northern world. Had one of them survived here, in this cave?

Tara stood hurriedly and stretched her wings wide. She reared back and was about to let fly with another stream of molten fire when the creature let forth a cry of its own.

"Rreeeeeeawrrrrr!"

Tara stopped and stood perfectly still. Then another sound came, calmer and less desperate.

"Meow."

Tara breathed more fire at the ceiling and looked in the direction of the sound. This time, it illuminated the cave long enough to reveal that the shadow she'd seen before had been a trick of the light: What stood before her was no saber-toothed cat. It was a common tabby.

Well, not so common, actually.

"Argentus!" Tara exclaimed.

"In the fur," the cat replied, and Tara did a doubletake.

"You can talk?"

"No, but you can hear me," came the reply in Tara's mind.

Indeed, Argentus hadn't made a sound since his meowed greeting, but Tara understood him just fine. "You never talked to me like this before."

The cat meowed again and started purring. "Sure, I did. You just didn't know how to listen. I tend to get my message across best when things are quiet. Even then, most humans can't hear me because they're too busy listening to their own silly thoughts. What I have to say is far more interesting."

He was a cat, all right. Self-important to the point of being imperious. He closed his eyes and began diligently licking one paw. "I had a hard time finding you," he said. "You aren't as easy to track as a mouse. You fly. Like those cursed birds." His teeth chattered reflexively.

"Sorry," he said. "Bad habit."

"Why were you trying to find me?"

"To tell you that the old man is in trouble. They kidnapped him and then burned down the woods. I got out just in time."

"Then he's all right?"

"I don't know." He turned his attention to his chest, rough tongue curling under his chin as he bowed his face forward and then pulled back with a great deal of determination.

"This is hard work," he said.

"You'll get furballs in your stomach."

"You don't think I know that?"

"Sorry."

"I *am* a cat, you know. I've had experience with these things."

"Sorry," Tara repeated, then changed the subject. "I heard a voice in my sleep. I think it was a message from E.O., but it sounded like a woman. I can't explain how I know, but it *felt* like it came from him."

Argentus stopped grooming and looked at Tara. She

could barely see him in the dark.

"What was this woman's name?"

"I don't know," Tara began. Then, inexplicably, a name came into her head. "Elyrian," she blurted out.

The cat meowed. "Elyrian," he said flatly. "She came to our home after you left, just before all these things started happening."

"Who is she?"

"A witch. A shade. A goddess. Maybe *the* goddess. Something not of this world. I tried to tell E.O. this, but he wouldn't listen to me, as usual. He didn't listen when I tried to warn him about the soldiers at the door, either. He thinks he's so smart."

"He *is* smart," Tara protested.

"Then he should listen to his cat." Argentus hurrumphed.

"You sound just like him, you know." Tara laughed.

The cat went back to grooming himself, more diligently this time, pretending he hadn't heard. After a moment, he said, "Why are you just sitting here in the dark?"

Tara lowered her head slightly. "I don't know what else to do. E.O. sent me to find a way to save the forest, and now the forest has been destroyed anyway. I failed in my mission."

"What if your mission isn't exactly what you thought it was? What if it isn't over? What if you haven't failed?"

The voice had not come from Argentus, who had

stopped grooming again. Tara couldn't hear any sound at all coming from his direction and concluded that he must be sitting at attention. Listening.

"Did you hear that?" she said.

"Yes."

"It was that woman's voice again." Tara sent a fireball rocketing upward that illuminated the entire cavern, but there was no sign of anyone else there.

"What *is* my mission, then?" Tara asked.

The woman's voice was silent, but she heard an echo of the earlier voice, " ... inside you. ..."

"Long Dashi told me my mission was to distract the nations from warring against one another," she said.

"You can still do that," Argentus said, his demeanor calm again. He yawned in the darkness.

"Well, if E.O. is still alive, it's worth continuing for his sake," Tara replied.

"That's the spirit. Now, give me a ride out of here, will you? I don't want to make my pads any more callused than they already are from walking such a long way looking for you!" He hurrumphed again. "You might want to remember your way back here," he added. "You wouldn't want to leave *that* behind." He was obviously gesturing toward something, but it was too dark for Tara to see what he might be talking about.

Whatever it was, she wasn't worried about it now. She was more worried about finding E.O. and making sure he was safe, and about fulfilling her mission. She had made a promise to Long Dashi, and even if it made little difference, she supposed it was still a promise worth keeping.

She felt the cat climb onto her back and curl up between her wings. Was he kneading her?

16

Siege

ing Balathorn wasn't happy about inviting Aelfric into his kingdom, but he didn't think he had much choice. The land had been in an uproar since the appearance of the beast or monster or demon. Depending on who was describing it, it was either a gigantic bat with talons like an eagle's, a gargoyle that threw down lighting from its wings, a shooting star that had taken on the form of a phoenix or a winged snake that shot flames from its nostrils.

The shepherds and cowherds had brought their flocks in from the fields, hoping to protect them from the menace overhead. The streets and the marketplace were all but deserted as men stayed indoors, hoarding their stores and keeping themselves out of danger.

Farmers had come to petition the king for relief from

their taxes, and others were refusing to pay outright, saying they couldn't raise any money if they couldn't sell their produce at the market.

The king refused such petitions, but he didn't know how long he could keep doing so before his subjects rose up in open revolt. Half his army, itself consisting mostly of conscript farmers, had deserted. He needed to do *something* to reassure the citizens that they were safe from whatever it was that had destroyed the woodland. Aelfric had offered assistance, and Balathorn didn't see how he could refuse it. Perhaps this Aelfric was different than Wyriven. Perhaps he would honor the truce. Balathorn knew better than to count on this, but given his desperate position, he didn't have many options.

Those who remained in his army, however, didn't like the idea of working with foreigners, and it wasn't long before any hopes that Balathorn had concerning an amicable arrangement came crashing down.

It happened after midnight, at the changing of the night watch. When Aelfric's men came in at the end of their shift, they attacked the home guard in an ambush, slaughtering dozens of men, but not before the alarm went up and reinforcements from Balathorn's contingent came running. Even with their numbers depleted by desertion, they outnumbered the foreigners slightly, and once the element of surprise was eliminated, the two sides fought each other on relatively even terms.

Swords were drawn, and metal clashed. Shouts rose

into the night and blood was spilled. And amidst it all, a giant shadow appeared in the night sky, lit up by a sudden burst of flame that exploded in a blazing stream just a few feet above their heads. The war cries gave way to shouts of panic and dismay as the two sides turned their attention from one another to the threat that had appeared in the sky. The monster flew west of the city, then wheeled and came back at them, diving sharply and exhaling another burst of fire that singed the hair on the backs of two dozen necks. Some of the men dove to the ground, others ran to the ramparts and, grabbing their bows, aiming for the sky.

The creature turned in the east and flew directly for them, not breathing fire this time but pulling up directly overhead and flapping its giant wings so forcefully that they were driven backward. Arrows flew but were wildly off target, caught in the gusting air and falling to the ground harmlessly behind the men who had fired them.

"What *is* that thing?" someone cried.

"They told me it was a myth!" someone from Aelfric's forces shouted.

"That myth is going to kill us all!"

Some of the men ran in terror, but more strengthened their resolve to defend the city against the monster. Banding together, easterner and westerner alike trained their arrows on the beast that assailed them, united against their common enemy, determined to repel it.

"To the catapults!" someone cried, and men ran to a pair of wooden mechanisms designed to hurl giant stones into the sky. These were drawn back, set and released, but the sky-demon was too quick for them, dodging them before they even got close and answering each volley with a stream of fire that sent men running. The catapults themselves were set ablaze and abandoned, but other men continued firing arrows into the night sky, hoping to find their mark. The target was quick and agile, but it was also big. They would only need a few arrows to bring it down, if their aim was true.

But the creature had other ideas. It whirled and banked, dived and rose, sending fire down at them that scattered the men but somehow never set them afire. Had they noticed this, they might have concluded that the monster was merely trying to scare them, not hurt them. But men seldom notice such things in the heat of battle. All they

134

notice is the enemy in front of them and their own drive to eliminate that enemy.

The beast changed direction and pulled back, away from the ramparts. Was it flying erratically? Some of the soldiers took to horseback and rode out of the city gates, following the main road as they pursued their quarry into the surrounding countryside. But as they raised their bows and nocked their arrows, the creature swung turned back toward them and sprayed a fountain of flame down across their path. The steeds reared up, some of them throwing their mounts, and the other riders turned their steeds around and headed at a gallop back toward the city. In their wake, fields of wheat and rye and oats on both sides of the caught fire, sending smoke and embers flying into the air.

Having set her assailants to flight, the sky demon banked off suddenly eastward and disappeared westward toward the dark horizon.

● ● ●

The next day, men in command of the two opposing armies met to seal a new pact between them: There would, indeed, be an end to hostilities between their lands, at least until the threat had been eliminated. This agreement was ratified then and there by Balathorn; Aelfric, sensing that his men might desert him if he failed to go along, also assented when news of the encounter reached him.

Among those present when Balathorn strode into the public square and set his signet to the truce was a man of some years, who carried a staff and was slightly bent in posture. No one noticed him, because he had a knack for blending into the background, even when he wasn't wearing a disguise.

The crowd cheered its approval when the truce was sealed, and Balathorn proclaimed, "We will do whatever is necessary to protect our kingdom from the ravaging sky hunter. We will bring it down from the heavens; we will destroy the threat to our lands!"

The man with the staff smiled slightly and nodded, then turned and disappeared through the crowd and out of the city.

17

Retreat

ara's head pounded and swirled. She struggled to fly straight, trying to remember the way back to the cave. She had left Argentus at the edge of the now-charred woodland before she had launched her attack, hoping that he might be able to find E.O. She had taken care not to wound any of the men defending the city.

Death and injury were not part of her mission. Once before, she had killed riders in anger for shooting at her, and she had promised herself she would not do it again. Her mission was to create fear, not death. The kind of fear that would motivate men to join together rather than tear one another apart. *That* was her mission.

Long Dashi had explained it to her thus: "Men will

take up arms against one another for any reason. They wage war over land. They wage war over gold. They wage war because they imagine that their gods command it, even though they themselves are the ones who command it and defile the names of their gods by their claiming their sanction.

"It is not the reason that is important, but the conflict. Men thrive on it. It is no use trying to dissuade them from it, for even among those who cherish peace, a leader will always arise to compel them to it. The best that can be done is to channel their aggression away from one another and toward a common goal.

"This is what you must do. You must give them a reason to hate someone other than their fellow human being. You will become the object of their hatred, the reason they must stop fighting one another and work together in common cause. You will become the enemy in their own minds, manifest in the skies above them."

But although Tara had kept her vow not to hurt any more of the humans, they had made no such vow toward her. Their arrows had been shot with the clear intent to bring her down; more than that, to destroy her. The archers had not succeeded — at least, they had not known of their success. They had not seen it when their arrows found their mark, embedding themselves in their clearest target: the two massive wings Tara used to keep herself aloft.

One of the arrows had embedded itself in the skin just above her right shoulder, and another had lodged near the center of her left wing. The initial stabbing pain of the first had become a shooting pain, radiating all up and down the span of her wing. In panic and frustration, she had bitten at it, but she had only succeeded in breaking off the shaft, while the shiny black obsidian arrowhead burrowed deeper into her shoulder every time she moved it. The other wing had been torn straight through, the half-connected pieces of skin flapping in the wind, making it difficult to keep on the same

heading — or even to stay aloft. The harder she flapped, the worse the tear became, and the more blood flowed from it. She knew she could not stay in the air much longer, but she didn't want to set down on open land, for fear that she might be attacked.

She had to make it back to the cave somehow and hope that Argentus could reach E.O. She knew he could help her, if anyone could. But part of her didn't want him to find her, because she feared putting him in any more danger. He had already lost his woodland home because she had failed to return in time. She did not wish to be the cause of any more sorrow for her friend.

Just as she thought she could go no farther, Tara

caught sight of the cave where she had taken shelter before her midnight flight. Relieved, she went in for a landing, nearly tripping over her own feet as her wings all but failed her. The pain in her right shoulder had grown more severe — a continual throbbing soreness — and her left wing felt numb.

She staggered into the cave and went several more steps before she nearly collapsed onto the ground, breathing hard from the exertion it had taken to keep herself in the air. Once again, she heard that tinkling-jangling sound when she lay down.

She felt something underneath her but, too exhausted to pay it any heed, she fell asleep.

• • •

As she tossed and turned fitfully in the depths of a dream, Tara kept hearing the tinkling sound. The throbbing pain of her wounds wouldn't allow her to get comfortable, try as she might. At last, the dream sleep fell away and she awoke, a flicker of candlelight tickling the back of her eyelids.

Her eyes snapped open and she jerked her head upward, sending a stabbing pain through her shoulder.

She heard a gasp and the sound of feet and saw the flame from the candle bob and weave through the darkness, moving backward. The candle was borne, Tara saw, by a small, wiry man with dark hair, darker eyes and a beard that fell somewhere between stubble and scruffy, matted growth.

He stopped a few steps away from her and kept his

distance, but did not retreat.

"Be warned, foul demon," he said in a whisper that was almost a hiss. "I deal with all thieves the same, be they man or beast."

"Thieves?" Tara winced and stifled a groan of pain. The throbbing was worse now.

The man was, naturally, startled to hear her speak the common tongue (or speak at all, for that matter). He lost his composure for a moment, but regained it once his eyes returned to the ground where Tara was seated.

"Yes, thieves!" He said urgently. "That" — he pointed to it with a long and narrow finger — "belongs to me."

Tara looked down and saw beneath her, spread out on the floor of the cavern, a pool of gold coins that glistened in the candlelight. Mingled in among them were rubies, emeralds, amethyst, pearls and crystals, along with platters and goblets and bejeweled adornments, all of them gold. This was what had made the jangling sound as she'd fallen asleep.

"If this is yours," she said, "why did you leave it here unattended? If you value it so much, shouldn't you have kept it with you?"

"Because of highwaymen and thieves like you!" He turned his long finger toward Tara now, accusingly. "This cave was safe — until you intruded!"

"You are the intruder. I have as much right to be here as you do." A wisp of smoke escaped her nostrils as she gritted her teeth against the pain. That pain was eating away at whatever patience she had for this small man; she just wanted to be left alone so she could sleep. "I do not believe your story. If you were a gentleman, you would not have come skulking about here to disturb my sleep." She glowered at him, her eyes flashing in the candlelight, and she snorted. "You haven't even bothered to introduce yourself, as is proper."

It was not as though Tara had been through many formal introductions. Apart from Long Dashi and Long Pengyou, she had no experience with meeting people. But E.O. had told her how people were expected to act in such situations, and the man in front of her was definitely not acting that way.

"Who are you?" She demanded, cranking her neck forward toward the little man, which induced him to retreat another step.

"Hor..." He paused, then blurted out, "Horatius Benatticus."

"Well, Horatius Benatticus, I don't think this treasure ever belonged to you. I believe *you* are the thief here. And since the real owner isn't present, it's mine now."

The little man howled in rage, drew a sword that he carried on his leather belt and started to rush at her.

Tara sprayed a warning shot of flame across his path,

and he jumped back with a high-pitched cry.

"It's mine now," she repeated, forcing her voice lower into something like a growl — rendered all the more menacing by the pain behind it. "Leave now, and don't come back, or you'll find me here guarding it and less willing to put any space between you and my fire."

She punctuated her warning with another burst of flame, and this time the man turned tail and went running from the cave as fast as he could. She stared at the darkness toward the cave opening until she was satisfied he wasn't coming back, then laid her head down again and lapsed into slumber once more.

● ● ●

The next time she awoke, Tara noticed it wasn't as dark as before. But it wasn't daylight yet, either. A faint blue glow was emanating from somewhere just around the corner.

Curious, she rose and found she could no longer lift her wings. The moment she'd stopped using them, they had become stiff, and now she had to drag them over the cave's rough stone floor to find the source of the light.

When she rounded a corner, she saw it: The glow was coming from a woman, whose face seemed to shimmer like the surface of a pond kissed softly by a gentle breeze. On her back was a purple shawl with gold trim, the hood of which framed those shimmering features that seemed smooth as fine glass. Grey eyes peered out at her, and she nodded slightly to acknowledge Tara's arrival, but her expression did not change.

When she spoke, Tara knew her voice: It was the same voice that had spoken to her in that dream, the dream she'd felt sure had been sent by E.O.

"You are hurt," the woman said.

Tara nodded, and winced in pain as she did so. It seemed as if every part of her body shared the pain she felt in her wings. "Can you help me?"

The woman shook her head sadly. "I fear not. I am a shaper, not a healer. Those skills are not mine to share."

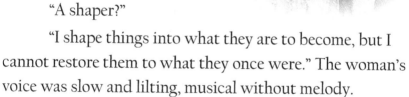

"A shaper?"

"I shape things into what they are to become, but I cannot restore them to what they once were." The woman's voice was slow and lilting, musical without melody.

"Perhaps my wings will heal, if I rest them for a time." Tara's voice was hopeful, but something tugging at her from within told her that hope was false.

The woman confirmed it, shaking her head again.

"You know E.O.," Tara said.

"We are acquainted."

"Will he be ... is he all right?"

The woman nodded. "He is well."

"Then perhaps he can heal …"

"No," the woman said. "Your wounds are beyond his ability, and you would only endanger him by your presence. Remember what Long Dashi told you."

"How did you know …?" Tara cocked her head, but the woman remained silent, so she asked another question: "Will I die here, then?"

The woman smiled for the first time. It was barely perceptible, but it was a smile, nonetheless. "You need not, unless you wish it," she said. "I cannot heal you, but I can shape you — make you into that which you were meant to be, now that your mission here is done."

"How?"

"Your wounds will soon fester, and the defilement will spread to the rest of your body," she said. "You must agree to relinquish your wings; this alone can spare you. The cost is great, but the reward will be your life."

Tara's eyes widened. It had taken so much effort for her to learn to fly, and she had taken so much pride in discovering how to do so. She had overcome her fear of falling and had ascended to the heavens, soaring through the clouds, the mist on her skin and the sun in her face when she broke clear into the open sky.

But the pain was not easing, and whenever she tried to lift her wings, it multiplied.

"How will I continue my mission?" she asked. "The

men will forget me and go back to fighting one another."

The woman closed her eyes and tilted her head. "Men will always fight one another," she said. "But these men, for a good many years, will be consumed by their fear of you, whether you appear again or not. Such was the terror you wrought that they brought their flocks and herds in from the field to protect them, fearing that you might attack them from the sky. No, the truce to which they agreed will hold, I am certain, at least for this generation, and many lives that might have been lost will be spared. The tales they tell of you will pass from story into legend, and it will be hundreds of years before they are forgotten — if they ever are. Long Dashi was right to have entrusted you with this task. You have done well."

Tara groaned, half in agony and half in sorrow. "Without my wings, I will not be able to flee when they hunt for me. They will find me, and even with my fire, I will be unable to defeat them."

The woman's eyes flashed with a brighter spark of the blue glow that emanated from her face. "You leave that to me," she said. "I can shape you. I promise, it will be painless. And when it is done, you will be safe. You have earned that much and more for the sacrifice you have given. I will take you away from this place."

"What should be done with this?" She nodded toward the gold coins and other treasure strewn across the floor if the cavern.

The woman answered with a question. "Do you know

who owns it?"

Tara shook her head.

"Then, what do you suggest?"

Tara thought a moment. "Perhaps it should be given to those who lost their livelihood in the fires I set upon them — the ones whose crops were destroyed when I assailed their city."

The woman nodded. "An excellent idea. I will see to it."

"Where will you send me?" Tara asked. "Will I ever see E.O. again?" But the woman answered only with a firm admonition: "Close your eyes."

Tara was scared, the way she had been scared when she was learning how to fly. But maybe this was just another thing to learn. Maybe the strange woman who had come to her here in the cave could be trusted. In any case, what choice did she have? The throbbing pain in her right wing was nearly unbearable now. She could not endure it much longer.

She closed her eyes. And when she opened them again, everything was different.

18

Transforming

.O. Spinesetter, Esq. was at peace. He didn't have his chair to rest in. He didn't have his books to read. It seemed like ages since he'd had a good cup of tea, but the new peace that had arisen between the two kingdoms was holding, and that in itself seemed a marvel. Yes, his woodland home was gone, but he had some seeds in his pocket — spruce, elm, alder, larch — and he resolved that he would plant them. He would not live long enough to see them grow tall and strong, as the trees of his own woodland had been, but younger men and women would come to enjoy them, and their daughters, and their daughters' sons after them.

There was but a single pang of sorrow deep in his breast, and it was no small thing. He missed Tara. And

Argentus. He had never been much for human company, but these two had been his companions, had accepted him — gruff exterior and all — had loved him for who he was. And he had loved them, too. He still did.

As he sat in a charred meadow surrounded by blackened tree trunks that touched the sky, he saw the first new shoots breaking through the earth's surface beneath him. He heard the song of a single lark, the first sign of life returning to the land, and he missed his friends even more.

As if on cue, a silver-grey tabby with ice-blue eyes approached from behind him and climbed up his tunic, onto his shoulder. He hadn't heard Argentus approach, so he jumped at the feeling of the padded paws on his back. Argentus managed to hang on without digging his claws too deeply into E.O.'s skin, then curled up around E.O.'s neck and started purring.

"Long time," the cat said, and E.O. was even more startled at hearing the feline's voice in his mind than he had been at feeling him land full-force on his back.

"You can ... speak?" he said.

"Not like you can," came the reply. "But you've figured out how to listen. Now that you don't have all those books and worries and studies to distract you. Your mind is clear, and you can actually hear for a change. It's about time."

E.O. chuckled. "I didn't know it was as easy as that," he said.

"It is."

"So I see. Have you seen Tara?"

The cat meowed and jumped off E.O.'s shoulder into his lap. He began kneading the wizard's belly and continued purring.

"Not since before the truce," he said. "But I trust she is well. She can take care of herself without our help now."

E.O. sighed. "I suppose you're right. She's all grown up."

"What will you do now?" the cat asked. "Write more books?"

"The woman who came to visit us? Elyrian? She told me there's a book inside me that's already written. I think I'll start reading that one."

"How do you think it will end?" the cat asked. "I'm curious, you know."

"Yes, I know," E.O. chuckled softly. "But I won't know any better than you until I read it. She said I wrote it before I was born, but I've forgotten where the story takes me. I guess I needed Tara to help remind me to go looking again."

"We both needed Tara," the cat said. "And she needed us."

But the old man closed his eyes to the bright sun and fell asleep. In a dream he opened the book he had written so many years ago, and read it from cover to cover. Then he wrote a few notes on the final page before he closed it.

When at last he put it down, he woke up again, but he wasn't where he had been before. He was back in the woodland as he'd known it, and he knew he'd never leave that place again.

• • •

When Tara opened her eyes, she was greeted by a pair of familiar faces. Long Dashi looked down at her, with Long Pengyou at his side. Both smiled when they saw she had awakened.

She sat up straight. "How did I get here?" she asked.

"We don't know," Pengyou said excitedly. "We went to one night as usual, and when we woke up, here you were. You've been sleeping here for a fortnight. We were afraid you might never wake. When we offered you food and drink, you would open your mouth to accept it, but you never once opened your eyes."

"You have accomplished your mission," Long Dashi said. It was not a question, but a statement.

"I suppose I have," Tara said. "The woodlands were lost, but the war of the fire flowers is over. There is peace."

"Precisely as I had hoped," Dashi exclaimed. "Well done, Tara! But ... what happened to your wings?"

Tara looked down at herself, first at one side and then the other. Where her wings had been before, there was now only perfectly healthy skin and a short pair of arms. Or legs. There was no sign of any injury; it was as if she had always been this way.

"They were injured," she said slowly. "By the arrows

152

men sent flying at me. There was a woman. She said she couldn't heal me, but that she could ... shape me."

"She must have sent you here because she feared men would hunt and kill you for what you had done," Dashi said thoughtfully.

"But how could she have brought me here?"

"I don't know. But there are many things I don't know. This is just one more of them!" He laughed, and Tara and Pengyou laughed with him.

"Do you know her?" Tara asked when their laughter had subsided.

"I'm not sure. In a manner of speaking, I think we all do."

Tara nodded. "What will happen now?"

"Well, I think we had better let you get some rest, but when you're feeling up to it, I think a parade is in order!"

"A parade?"

Dashi chuckled. "Much has changed since you left us so short a time ago," he said. "Look around you. You are not in the bamboo forest."

Tara allowed her eyes to wander and realized he was right. She was not in the bamboo forest at all, but in a great hall with a giant ceiling, from which hung banners and pennants in many festive colors. "Where are we?"

"The imperial palace," Dashi said with a wink. "After the fire flowers were taken, I began thinking: What if the men who stole them did not wish to use them in *your* land, but wished to remain here and seek to challenge the emperor? Our emperor has been a compassionate ruler, and there has been peace after many years of conflict; I could not allow him to continue in ignorance of this threat, so I traveled here to his palace to warn him.

"I gave him the fire flowers as a token of my trust, and he accepted them gratefully. He promised he would not use them to wage war on any other nation, but would employ them as I always intended: as a means of joyfully celebrating all that is good in life. Not only did he keep his word, but he named me his highest advisor.

"When you ... arrived ... I told him of your mission and that it must have been successful because, well, here you are! He insisted that the moment you awoke, we should send word to him that he might plan a parade in your honor. Such courage, he said, would inspire the entire land to remain at peace.

"It is almost the feast of the new year. You woke up just in time!"

Tara bowed her head. "I don't know," she said shyly. "I do not deserve this honor."

"The very fact you just said that proves you do!" Dashi said. "Besides, would you dare to disappoint the emperor?"

"I suppose not," Tara said, her face brightening.

19

Completion

 few days later, Tara took part in the great parade, as everybody cheered and fire flowers exploded overhead. She was so happy that she didn't just walk, she danced, and she found that she enjoyed the dancing as much as flying, perhaps even more.

Ramphy and all the other ramphys learned of the festivities and flew down from the high Himalayas to celebrate, circling overhead and dancing themselves among the exploding fire flowers.

Tara saw them there and wanted to fly up and say hello, but without her wings, this was no longer possible, and they dared not descend to greet her. She thought, however, she saw her friend Ramphy wave goodbye as he and the others disappeared in the southwestern sky. She never saw them again, nor did anyone else, not even the monks of Tibet.

When the festival was concluded, Tara was allowed to stay in the palace as an honored guest, and there she remained for the rest of her days. She took to the water and learned to swim, finding to her delight that her new form enabled her to challenge the waters at any depth and in whatever manner they manifested themselves, whether as sea or river, lake or ocean. She became renowned for this, to such an extent that she was lauded for her mastery of the waters, and some even claimed she could calm the seas and quiet the rains.

To this day, at every new year's celebration in Zhongguo, a parade is held in honor of the only dragon, whose part is now played by citizens who don a costume in her likeness and dance beneath a sky of exploding flowers. Even now, though her story has dimmed from the memories of most, the entire land celebrates the courage of Tara and the good luck she brought the land on her arrival.

The names of her friends were remembered, too. Long Dashi's name came to mean "dragon master," and Long Pengyou was remembered as "dragon friend."

In the west, she was remembered differently, as the sky demon farmers always feared would return to feast on their flocks and ravage their land with molten fire.

It never happened, but they never quite stopped

worrying that it might, and although they returned to warring against one another — just as Elyrian said they would — fewer people died because they feared the return of the dragon whose tale had become legend on the tongues of every man in Britannia, which became the land of the Angles and Saxons, then a great empire that spanned the globe.

When men from that empire came upon what had once been Zhongguo — a land, now known as China that had been largely removed from their notice for centuries — they marveled that they shared with the people of that land the legend of a dragon. Their own, winged; the Chinese dragon wingless. But similar in so many other respects. They never guessed that there had only been one of these creatures in all of history, and that they had both shared in the gifts she bestowed upon them.

When Tara reached the end of her days, she closed her eyes, just as E.O. had, and found herself reading a book of her own. When she reached the end of it, she awoke and found herself back in the woods of Britannia, with E.O. sipping his tea and Argentus purring softly in his lap.

"We've been waiting for you," the wizard said. "We missed you."

A single tear ran down Tara's long nose. She was with her old friend at last. She had at last come home again.

Epilogue

 hese are the notes E.O. Spinesetter made at the end of the book he opened when he closed his eyes that final time — recalling at last all the things that he had known at the beginning.

What I did not understand, and what men in general do not understand, is that the book within us is not like a book one reads at bedtime before falling asleep, then picks up again the next evening.

It is a book that was written before time, and which is continually being written as time passes. Its beginning and ending are certain, but not fixed.

If you find this difficult to grasp, you are not alone. It is only now that I myself am removed from the dominion of time, that I can see such things from the proper perspective. From within time itself, the view is always dim and uncertain, like a flickering candle at the far edge of one's vision.

Only the wise ones see even this much of it. The ones who can hear the gentle breeze above the sound of war and fury. The ones who can see the cause of illness past the horrors of its symptoms. The ones who can understand the tongue of the cat and the owl and the otter — although each one is unspoken.

Caught in the maelstrom of time, such things are easily missed. Even those who glimpse them cannot share them, even though they long to do so.

Unable to describe what words cannot contain, yet unwilling to accept such limitation, these wise ones play the part of fools. Forsaking the book that is within them, they dedicate themselves to producing copies with pen and parchment — copies they deem perfect and sacred. Yet these are, at best, pale shades of the original and, at worst, mere products of their own imaginations.

These books, set as if in stone, become judges and tyrants of the people, demanding their blind service instead of serving them as the true book does.

The true book is the product of each man's journey, a map to guide him and a story to be told when he is done. It is the product of all of us together, striving for those things we hold in common with one another, as well as with the deer and the bear and the oak tree and the sparrow.

The true book binds us together, while the false copies set us one against another to squabble over details that obscure the true book's message.

In my quest to discover meaning in these copies, I neglected to listen to the cat and the owl and the otter (most especially my own feline companion, who tried so hard to get me to listen).

It took a creature they called a dragon to bring me understanding, to teach me the wisdom I had forgotten ... and all while I presumed to be teaching *her*.

She was the only dragon, and this is her story, contained here within my own true book. Whether those in the realm of time can hear it will depend on their ability to listen to their own stories, which might seem, perhaps, a little different. Yet it is in hearing such differences that we find our common voice.

What to one may be a myth, to another is life and certainty. Perception is the gateway to reality, and so it shall always be. This is what I had forgotten and which now, in this place beyond time, I at last remember. It is my hope that others remember, too ... or find their own dragons to remind them.

𝕿𝖍𝖊 𝕰𝖓𝖉

What follows is another story, a myth perhaps, or a truth as told by a man who lived in another time and another place. In this tale, there is more than a single dragon, and the dragons whose story is told on the pages ahead are of a very different sort.

To say any more will spoil the story; it is best to let it speak for itself. In part, it will seem familiar, but the whole of it has yet to be told.

Until now...

Ѳeorge & the Дragon:
Дhe Цntold Ѕtory

anta Claus. The tooth fairy. The boogieman. During my childhood, the things I believed in seemed to slip away from me one by one. No matter how tightly I clung to them, there was always something that burst the bubble of what I discovered, a few years short of puberty, to be pure fantasy.

Such ideas, I came to realize, had been planted in my

mind by grownups who had abandoned their own beliefs in such things, with equal reluctance, before I was born. They couldn't look each other in the eye and admit to accepting them, so they passed the beliefs on to me and other kids so they could believe in them vicariously through us.

This is how fairy tales survive for centuries while the historical deeds of real men and women who lived and died and made a difference in the world get forgotten. It's how kids get disillusioned with their parents, and with the stories they hear in childhood.

Do I sound bitter?

Well, if you lose your mother at the age of seven and you find out years later that it had something to do with one of these fairytales, then maybe you'll understand. Try growing up without a mom — and with a father who hid the truth from you — and tell me you wouldn't be bitter about it, too.

As I grew older, like most kids, I left those fairytales behind. Over time, they faded into the forgotten corners of my childhood with the memories of family Christmases and kindergarten and Cub Scouts.

But one conversation always stuck with me. It was something my grandpa taught me; I'm not sure whether he'd heard somewhere or made up himself: "There's no better way to conceal a lie than behind a thousand truths, and there's no better way to conceal the truth than behind a thousand lies." Considering what's happened since, I don't think he shared this wisdom by accident. He was, after all, Mom's father, and

I suspect he knew what was going on. He just didn't want to make things worse by telling me. I don't blame him. I'm not sure I wouldn't have made the same decision myself.

The saying has to do with Mom. And those fairytales. You see, I've come to believe that the lies we call children's stories, the ones that have been passed down to us for generations, have a very real purpose. They aren't just meant to entertain us until we outgrow them, and they're supposed to distract us from learning the truth.

Dragons are real.

And they're not at all what they appear to be, because the stories about dragons themselves are largely lies, meant to cover up humanity's shame at what we've done.

Oh, it's no secret — according to the stories, at least — that human beings drove dragons to the brink of extinction, just as we did with the passenger pigeon and the black rhino, and the Tasmanian tiger, which died out for the same reason: It was hunted and exterminated to protect livestock.

The same might be said for dragons, but, I learned, dragons were different. Humankind declared war on them hundreds of years ago, during the Dark Ages, long before we eradicated the passenger pigeon or hunted the black rhino into oblivion.

But there's something about the comparison that doesn't quite fit. The human population was much smaller back then, and we didn't have hunting rifles or elephant guns at our disposal. So how could this have happened? How could men, armed with nothing but swords and spears and longbows, have conquered flying beasts that breathed fire and rode the wind on wings that made condors seem like sparrows?

They couldn't have, obviously ... which is why it's easy to dismiss the stories of the dragons' demise as just more children's fairytales. In fact, that's just what I did. Until I found the manuscript, that is.

It was one of the few things my grandpa left me, sealed in a leather folder inside a mahogany box. It has been almost twenty years since Mom disappeared, and my father never told me what happened. Mom had been special, and not just because she was *my* mom. She was the kindest person I knew, and fiercely protective of me. Dad had a violent temper, and he'd yell and scream and throw things when he got bent out of shape, but she never let him lay a finger on me. She always stood between him and me, even if it meant putting herself in harm's way. He never hit her — not that I saw — but I know he resented something about her, though I never figured out just what.

There were a couple of other things about Mom that made her unique. She had slightly webbed fingers, which she used to joke about, saying my grandpa was the creature from the black lagoon. (I knew this wasn't true, because he hated the water and couldn't even swim.) Then there was this weird birthmark she had on her neck that looked like three or four tiny leaves, one overlaying the other. She always seemed self-conscious about it and wore high-necked shirts or scarves to hide it.

Mom was the perfect mother. She read me bedtime stories, made me hot cocoa at Christmas and told my teachers at school to stop being so tough on me when I had a harder time learning to read than some of the other kids.

She was always there for me — until, one day, she wasn't.

Dad said she left and didn't tell him where she was going. I remember when the police came by the house to ask him about it, and I hid just around the corner in the bedroom to hear what he'd tell them. But he didn't tell them any more than he'd told me: She'd just left.

There was an investigation, and they kept the case open, but she never came back and they never found any body.

Just after she disappeared, though, I happened to see Dad burying something in the back yard. He saw me watching him, and he made me swear never to go nosing around there or he'd whup me. That scared me, but what scared me even more was what I might find there. Whuppin' or not, I didn't want to know.

My dad took charge of Mom's belongings — what she'd had before they got married — and I remember Grandpa shouting at him over it, saying some of those things were rightfully his. He didn't get anywhere with it, though. Dad was the surviving spouse, and she hadn't left a will, so the law said that stuff belonged to him.

But I don't think Dad realized that Grandpa had the manuscript — Dad probably never even knew it existed — and when he died at 46 of a heart attack, Grandpa let me move in with him for the next couple of years. Then Grandpa died, too, and left me a few things in his will: his old walking stick, which I'd loved to play with as a child; a few thousand dollars in savings bonds; and the key to the mahogany box where I found the manuscript.

It was a few pages long, laid on top of one another, all loose. The paper was cracked in some places and torn in others. There was something that looked like a small coffee stain in the corner of one of the pages, and in another place, it looked like it had been singed by a candle. It looked very old, but I think it must have been translated from an even earlier script, because it was written in the first person.

Some lines (I don't know how many) had been lost — torn away from the top of the first page and then again at the end, but it seemed like the rest was intact. I could tell you what was in it, but it would be easier just to read it for yourself. Here's what it said:

• • •

... In those days, I sojourned for a time in the city of Silene, which is in Libya, and it is there that I came upon Lucinda, a maiden from that city who was in great distress, for she dwelt apart from her people in a cavern twenty

leagues to the east. I happened upon the cavern quite by accident one day, as I was exploring the land at my leisure, and surprised her there while she was sleeping, a smooth stone as her pillow and a handful of straw as a blanket.

I startled her with my presence, and she rose quickly, taking two steps backward and making as if to flee into the cavern's darkness. But I besought her, assuring her that I would not harm her and that, should she wish it, I would depart straightaway.

Thereupon she hesitated, but shook her head slightly and bade me sit and rest a moment.

I did so, never once taking my eyes off the maiden. She

was tall and fair and beautiful, with dark silken hair and ruddy cheeks, and eyes that glistened in the sunlight that danced off a pool of water there within the cavern. She spoke not a word for the space of several moments, like a young deer standing and watching at a distance, fearful that a lion might suddenly appear.

Then, ever so slowly, her shoulders relaxed and her brow unfurrowed, and I could see that she was becoming more at ease in my company. Truth be known, I was instantly taken with her, and she warmed to me quickly as I spoke to her of the lands I had seen in my travels and the wonders I had beheld as a knight in service of true wisdom.

She spoke little of herself, which I thought strange, but when I rose to depart, she implored me not to forget her and, indeed, to visit her there often, as she was fated to tarry in this cavern until the next full moon.

I asked her why this must be, but she implored me: "Dear friend, speak to me of any other thing, but not of this, for I will breathe no word of it, even should you plead with me or threaten my life."

I wondered at these words of hers, but I did not press her, for it would not have been seemly to do so. Yet even so, they vexed me, for I wished more than almost anything to know how she had come upon this circumstance — more than anything, should I speak the truth, save that one day she might favor me with a kiss.

But she warned me: "Speak not of your visits to any man, lest you place yourself in danger, for this place is forbidden to my people. And when the moon next reaches its fullness, do not return here, but until then, be my succor."

So it was that I rode out each day to where she dwelt, taking with me palm dates and pomegranates and olives and wine to preserve her strength, for I had seen no source of sustenance in the cavern.

These she gratefully accepted and, for many hours, we spoke of my travels, her childhood, my dreams and her regrets. And she was with me, and I with her, for we loved each other. But though we spoke of all things dear to our hearts and to each other — our lips never dared touch upon the one thing I wished most earnestly to know: how she had come to be exiled there.

Although I had sworn by my honor that I should not ask her of this, I had not vouchsafed that I should refrain from asking another. Therefore, when I returned to the city one evening, I sought out an inn where men would congregate after sunset, my intention being to pose this question discreetly to some among them. One I came upon supplied the answer, which apparently was commonly known in the city:

The maiden was, he told me, the daughter of the king, and her exile to the cavern was the result of a cruel trick of fate. There dwelt in that cavern, the man said, a great dragon whose wings were wider — each one of them — than the building in which we were taking our leisure. The dragon's maw was filled with teeth sharper than a makhaira, and from the depths of its belly issued forth blue flame hotter than any from a blacksmith's forge.

The beast had departed the region for a time to raid the flocks of the shepherds beyond the city, but would return at the full moon. An oracle had revealed to the king that it could only be satiated by human blood and flesh, so he had called all the city together to cast lots as to who would sacrifice himself for the good of the people. The lot was drawn in secret by the king himself, and it had fallen to his own daughter, Lucinda.

With great sorrow had the king acceded to the will of the fates and banished his daughter to the dragon's cavern, where she went willingly and agreed to stay without even a guard being set there, with her honor as a guarantee that she would fulfill that for which she was destined. To the whole city, she had become an example of self-sacrifice and heroism, for she had given herself freely to save them all, and for this they were ever grateful.

"Yet would it not be better," I asked the man, "if one should venture forth to that place and slay the dragon?"

But the man only laughed at me. "What is your name, stranger?" he asked me.

"Jurj," I said, telling him my name in Arabic.

"Well ... George, is it? ... did you not hear the description I gave of the beast? What hope has any man among us of slaying such a winged demon, which calls forth fire from its belly and could fly away from us before we could even raise a blade against it?"

I said nothing, but thought to myself what a coward this man was, not to even to consider the attempt, when Lucinda had set forth unarmed to face the dragon on his behalf.

"Thank you, Friend," I said. "You have enlightened me far more than you know."

It was then that I determined it would be I who would slay this dragon, though it would require that I break my vow to Lucinda herself and appear in the cavern at the next full moon. I procured the services of a certain smith to forge a sword for me long enough, I judged, to reach the beast yet light enough still to wield. I also purchased a spear that could be thrust with the hand or hurled like a javelin, should I be unable to approach the beast too closely.

When the time came, I saddled my horse and set forth, weapons in hand, resolute of purpose and determined that I should not return 'ere the beast was slain.

I came to the cave and found there an eerie glow between gold and silver, the beams from the full moon cascading down off the desert sandstone and in through a small opening overhead. Lucinda was nowhere to be seen, at which I was greatly relieved, for I had no wish to endanger her by confronting the beast in her presence.

But my relief vanished when I saw the great dragon itself lying curled 'round its own body in the center of the chamber. Scales in shades of from yellow to gold to dark brown covered the creature as it slumbered, shimmering soft in the moonglow. Rising and falling with each breath, they seemed to ebb and flow in ripples up and down its back as it rested content upon the cool earth. Its eyes were shut in soft repose, its face marked with a diamond shape of darker scales across the forehead, and more clustered around its cheeks, with the rest of its countenance marked in gold and something close to crimson.

Two great wings rested in folds across its back, the flesh there devoid of scales, yet leathery and thick. I had never seen anything so wondrous, and for a moment I doubted my intent: How could I slay such a breathtaking creature? Was this beast not also God's creation? And perhaps, in truth, the pinnacle of his work! I nearly lost myself in a reverie admiring it, but then it stirred, rolling slightly onto its side and bringing me back again to my senses. I caught my breath, then released it after a moment when I had assured myself its eyes were still closed, and that the great belly, covered with lighter orange and yellow scales, was now exposed, along with ...

Was it possible?

Yes! When the dragon turned, it revealed something held close to its breast, something not visible before, when its body was curled 'round about it: A large egg, azure in color like the evening sky, and sparkling with what seemed like tiny stars winking out from its surface. A reflection of the heavens, or so it seemed, far larger even than an ostrich egg and cradled in a nest of straw like a bird might make.

The beast had come here to make its nest. But if it were here, resting, and Lucinda was gone ... was it possible she had fled? No, this I doubted. She had vowed to offer her own life up to the beast for the good of the city, and I had no doubt of either her virtue or bravery in carrying out this task.

Was I too late?

Had the great dragon already taken her? Did it now rest there, its meal finished, in sated slumber?

This was the only conclusion my mind could reach, and in despair's stark certitude, I felt a rage boil up from inside me. Righteous and unholy at once, it flooded through my body, a thirst for vengeance — the Lord's prerogative, and yet, I must have it. Lucinda had been too precious to me not to seize it, and as I gazed upon the creature before me, its beauty seemed to vanish 'neath the hideous mask of my own great wrath.

I let forth a cry as I rushed forward, and it stirred,

opening its eyes. For a moment, I thought I recognized something behind those eyes, something familiar that, were it not for my fury, might have caused me to hesitate. But I was too consumed by my hatred at the beast for taking Lucinda from me to give my actions any pause. The slightest delay, and the beast would turn upon me. I had to strike.

Racing forward astride my steed with all the force that I could muster, I aimed my lance at its exposed breast, unprotected by the scales that covered the rest of it. My hand was steady and my aim was true, and I watched with satisfaction as my weapon plunged deep into the creature's body, calling forth a font of crimson from beneath the surface.

The dragon sent forth an anguished cry that shook the cavern from floor to ceiling, sending small stones cascading down the walls and rousing a handful of sleeping fruit bats that took to wing.

There was something in that cry that gave me pause — something almost human, as though the beast were crying, "No!"

Surely, I was imagining it.

I leaped down from my mount, blade drawn, and ran toward the creature's head, determined that I should show no mercy to the beast that had slain my Lucinda.

As its eyes looked up at me, dark and glistening, they seemed to be pleading with me silently to look deeper, to see something I was missing. But in my rage, I had no use for such pleas. I raised my sword and plunged it deep into the

176

dragon's throat, drawing forth from it a hideous gasp of agonizing pain and ... it almost seemed like, disbelief.

I drew back as the creature thrashed wildly about, not wishing to be caught in the fury of its death throes, and watched as its will to fight and then its very life drained out of the massive body. The shimmering scales grew dull, despite the moonlight, and the wings fell limp. At length, it curled up tight around the egg that it had been guarding, and drew its final breath.

I stood there for some moments, watching it, after that, sword still in hand but no longer raised, held in place by something — I knew not what. I was about to turn and take my leave when I noticed the dragon's body begin to stir again.

Was it alive still? How could this be?

But no — no breath issued forth from its nostrils, and no other sign of life could I see. Its body was ... shrinking. Changing into something else.

I stood, transfixed, as I witnessed this transformation, horror mixed with dawning recognition that welled up inside my breast as the dragon's body slowly became something else entirely. Some*one* else. Until, at last, there lay before me the bloodied and broken body of a naked woman.

My Lucinda.

Her arms wrapped tight around the egg that remained, as before, clutched tightly to her breast, almost as large as her own body.

What madness was this? What sorcery? What

enchantment?

I fell to my knees and crawled toward her, anguish replacing the rage that had driven me, all hope lost from my empty heart. *I had done this.* Unknowing, but it had been I, no demon-beast, who had killed my own true love. How was this possible? I lifted her head and cradled it in my arms, and I wept bitter tears for what I had lost that could never be regained.

The news would spread that I had slain the dragon, and I would be hailed as a hero far and wide for my presumed bravery. And yet I knew the truth of it, that I had slain the only woman I had ever loved. This was my punishment for usurping the wrath of God and claiming vengeance, but what punishment had Lucinda deserved? Were it not for the child she left me, I would have taken my own life, but I owed my daughter a life of her own, and I vowed that I should bring her up to know her mother, whose eyes and visage were reflected in her own. I swore that ...

• • •

That's where it ended, this story of Saint George and the Dragon that few others had ever read.

I wondered at the meaning of those last few lines. The writer hadn't mentioned anything about a child before then, and there didn't seem to have been enough time for Lucinda to have given birth. Perhaps George had adopted the child, but he spoke of it as if it were his own — his and Lucinda's together.

What did that mean?

I had no idea.

For a while, I thought about taking the manuscript to an expert, maybe a professor at the university or someone who knew something about the ancient Near East. But I decided, in the end, to keep the story to myself. It had been among Mom's belongings, and if she'd wanted to share it with the world, she would have. It wasn't my place to second guess her.

Besides, there were plenty of people who wouldn't want this story to come out — people who knew what they thought was the "true" story of Saint George and wouldn't want others reading this new version of the tale.

So, I kept the story to myself. I read and reread it every

night for a month, and when that month was over, I put it away and never looked at it again. I didn't need to, because I could have recited it from memory. For some reason I couldn't quite understand, it felt real to me. It wasn't like Santa Claus or the tooth fairy; it seemed like a real-life adventure that real people had lived. It didn't matter that its supposed author was a Roman soldier from the Middle East who became the patron saint of England more than a thousand years after his death. The words he'd written, no matter how unlikely, rang true.

I put the manuscript back in the mahogany box where I had found it, used the key to lock it and put it in a safe place. I took the key to the bank and put it in a safe deposit box, and I never had any desire to open the box again.

But something else kept gnawing at me. If that box had contained such an unexpected treasure, what might be hidden in the back yard, where I had seen my father burying something as a child? I hadn't seen what it was — he'd been almost done by the time I saw what he was doing — and I'd always been curious what he might have been hiding. My father was gone now, and I had no need to fear getting whupped if he caught me digging around out there. Still, just the idea of it gave me a knot in my stomach. It was as though I'd be breaking some important taboo ... or, more alarming, that I might find something I didn't want to see.

If the manuscript had taught me anything, though, it was that things weren't always what they seemed. If the story it contained was real — and I was convinced it was —

it meant that all the superstitious nonsense about Saint George saving the princess from a dragon had been all wrong. He hadn't saved her at all. He wasn't a hero or a noble champion, but a broken man who had tried and failed to save the woman he loved from a fearsome beast.

I'd continued to live in my childhood home after my father's death; I was alone there now, unmarried and without any real attachments. My girlfriend and I had broken up a month earlier, and we'd never reached the point of living together anyway. I'd had a roommate for a while — a friend of mine from college who smoked too much and paid too little rent (you never really know someone until you live with him, right?), so we'd parted ways around the first of the year. The house was quiet most of the time, except for the creaky moans it uttered when settling or the echoes of Merle Haggard or Def Leppard when I listened to some music.

On this particular day, I was playing Billy Joel — not so much to drown out the house's creaking as to muffle the voices in my head. My doubts. My fears.

I had gotten out of bed this morning determined that I was going to do this thing.

I walked down the stairs and out the sliding glass door into the back yard, where fog sat dangling from the sky in tendrils that reached the ground and seeped into the soil. The gray mist hung among the branches of some fig, orange and tangelo trees my father had planted out by the wooden fence. Once upon a time, he'd thought to harvest them, but he'd never gotten around to it; the fruit had fallen from their branches and lay rotting on the ground.

I unlocked the small metal shed at the side of the house, its door rusted at the hinges. Stepping into the cold, musty air, I pulled the chain at the entrance, but the light must have burned out. Fumbling around in the half-darkness, I stubbed my toe on an old push-mower and knocked over a rake that had been propped up against the wall before I found what I was looking for: a long spade shovel with a splintery wooden handle. Fortunately, I found some gloves lying on a sawhorse beside me; slipping them on, I took the shovel and went back outside.

The sun, peering out through the veil of morning mist, looked more like a blurred full moon as I crossed the moist grass and patches of soft, damp earth to where I'd seen my father digging so many years earlier. I knew the exact spot where he'd been kneeling that day, looking over his shoulder at me as I stood on the back porch and fixing me with a look that said, "You shouldn't be here. Forget you ever saw this." He told me much the same thing in words later on, but it was that look that stayed with me, and I knew exactly where he'd been when he had seen his young son standing there looking at him.

He'd been about three feet this side of the fig tree, which had lost all its leaves as autumn crept toward winter and stretched out with barren branches to embrace the fog like a long-absent consort.

The ground where I planted the point of my shovel was bare; no grass grew in a circle about six feet around —

and hadn't for as long as I could remember. It might have been that way before my father buried whatever he'd hidden down below, but something told me it hadn't been — that the grass had refused to grow there in the years since, its silent protest against any involvement in my father's deed.

The soil was compacted, and I had to push hard to get any purchase with the shovelhead, stepping on it with one foot and lifting my whole body off the ground as I thrust the point of it into the earth. It resisted, but I was able to dislodge a small half-shovelful of dirt and toss it aside.

I repeated the process.

And again.

The earth, disrupted, began to yield more readily, and my pace accelerated. I was half a foot down, then a foot, then two feet when I hit something. The scraping sound told me it was made of wood — maybe like the box that had contained the manuscript. But as I started removing more dirt, it was clear this box was a lot bigger. I kept digging and scraping the dirt aside and removing it as I went. It seemed the pine surface would never end. How on earth had my father managed to bury it by himself?

I remembered back to that day: He had dropped me off at my friend Jackie's house in the morning, but he'd forgotten to come get me, so I'd asked Jackie's parents to take me home. I'd walked through the living room, the kitchen and out onto the back porch — which is when I saw him. From the look of the box, he must have been at it the whole time I was gone.

I could tell by the position of the sun in the sky that it was nearly noon now, but the mist showed no sign of burning off. It would be one of those early winter days when the fog stayed put, an uninvited but stubborn guest.

By the time I was done clearing away the dirt, I had exposed a box that must have been twelve feet long and six feet wide.

A twist in my gut whispered what I feared might be inside, but I had to look.

It was nailed shut tight.

I went back to the toolshed and grabbed a crowbar, which I set in the narrow space where the lid was nailed to the side nearest me

and pried upward. The wood started to give way, then cracked and splintered.

I tried another space, repeating the process and, at last, was able to pry the lid loose enough that I could get down on my knees and raise it up. Fetid air wafted up from inside, along with a thin plume of dust. And there, in the darkness, lay a human skeleton, not a shred of flesh remaining on the bones, but wearing a dress I recognized from childhood. I hadn't seen it in years, let alone thought about it. But I'd tugged at the white lace hem of that now-dusty blue dress many times when I was a toddler, trying to get the attention of the woman who wore it.

Mom.

I bent over and started to sob, all the grief that I'd felt when she disappeared careening back into me. I'd known she was dead — I mean really known it, not just given up hope: We'd had a connection, the way mothers and their children often do, and I couldn't feel that anymore after the day she disappeared. Still, there was some part of me that thought she wasn't really in the ground somewhere; that she was alive, in some sense, even if it was only in my memories. The sight of her corpse lying there in a wooden box shattered that part of me, and I knew I'd never be able to piece it back together.

Dad had killed her. There wasn't any sign that her neck had been broken or that she'd been shot; it was as if she had just gone to sleep. But I knew my father had killed her; poisoned her, maybe, or put a pillow over her head while she was asleep. Still there on my knees, I balled up both fists and slammed them into the ground beside me until the knuckles started to bleed. I closed my eyes tight against the image of Mom lying there, but I could still see it against the back of my eyes, exactly the way she looked when I opened them up again.

What I had barely noticed, in my grief and shock, was that the box contained something other than her remains: There was a second box, set at my mother's feet, taking up most of the width of the larger box and measuring about four feet across. As I listened, I heard a sound coming from inside it, like an animal had become trapped there and was scratching or thumping at the wood, trying to get out.

I pulled the box out and set it aside on the ground, then closed my mother's burial box and shoveled the dirt back over it. I was grateful for the fog and the fact that we lived on a three-acre lot so no one would notice what was happening — just as no one had noticed when my father had buried her all those years ago.

I felt nauseated.

By the time I was done, I was dripping with sweat, despite the cool, wet day, the moisture of the fog and my perspiration mingling and running down across my forehead.

I picked up the smaller box and carried it into the house, setting it on the table. Not only had the scraping sound intensified, I could feel it move a little in my hands, jostling back and forth.

What could be inside?

Using the crowbar once again, I pried open the lid and took a step backward as my mind struggled to make sense of what I saw in front of me. There in that box was a gigantic cracked egg, its contents struggling to break free. This was impossible. It has been almost twenty years since Mom had disappeared — had died. Whatever was inside that egg must have survived for *nearly two decades*. No animal I'd ever heard of had a gestation period like that. How could it have survived?

The question was moot, though, because it *had*.

Whatever "it" was.

I knew I was about to find out.

Reaching into the box, I inserted two fingers into the gap where the shimmering azure shell had cracked, curled them under and pulled back. The shell peeled away easily, revealing a gap underneath. I tried to peer in, but I still couldn't see anything; the shell jostled around some more, and I heard a noise that sounded like an infant's cry.

Hurriedly, I peeled back some more of the shell, flaking it off piece by piece, until the cavity revealed its contents.

A little girl's blue eyes stared up at me, tufts and wisps of golden hair on her forehead and straggling down on either side of a round, cherubic face. Her little lips smiled, and she said something that sounded like "goo" as I picked her up and cradled her in my arms.

"Who are you?" I asked. "Where did you come from? How did you survive all that time in there, little girl?"

She lolled her head back, her eyes blinking against the sudden brightness as she tried to look around. She appeared for all the world like any other baby, except she lacked a belly button and had a strange odor that seemed a little like rotten eggs. Well, she had come from inside an egg, so that made sense, but still, this smell wasn't *exactly* like that, it was more like something else — it reminded me of the mineral hot springs resort at the edge of town that had closed down a couple of years back.

"What's your name, little girl?" I asked, knowing she couldn't answer.

But then, as I watched, the strangest thing happened: She laughed, and what seemed to be a puff of smoke came wafting up out of her open mouth. I looked closer, and saw a glow inside, a flash of something that was more than a spark but less than a flame ... coming from inside her nostrils.

I looked again at the fragments of eggshell. They were blue, the same color that the writer described in ... Was it possible? Had that little girl emerged from a *dragon's egg*? If so, where was the dragon? Unless ...

I looked down at the little face again, entirely human and smiling up at me, but there was something else about her — something I hadn't noticed the first time I looked at her. Between the fingers of each of her tiny hands was a flap of skin that made her look like she was related to the creature from the Black Lagoon. And there, on her neck, was my mother's same birthmark of little leaves.

I looked closer. Maybe not leaves. Maybe scales.

I cradled the little girl in my arms, realizing I wouldn't

be alone in the house anymore. I'd be sharing it with my sister, born a dragon like all the women in my mother's family, all the way back to George's beloved princess. And even if *she* was the dragon, it was *my* turn to do the protecting.

George may have gotten it wrong, but I'm going to get it right.

I know my family secret, and now that I do, I'm gonna make Mom proud of me.

Also by the Author

Works of Fiction

The Memortality Saga

Memortality

Paralucidity

Identity Break

Feathercap

Nightmare's Eve

Works of Nonfiction

Highway 99

Fresno Growing Up

Undefeated

The Phoenix Chronicles

The Osiris Testament

The Way of the Phoenix

The Gospel of the Phoenix

The Phoenix Principle

Forged in Ancient Fires

Messiah in the Making

Requiem for a Phantom God

Media Meltdown in the Age of Trump

𝕻raise for other works

"The complex idea of mixing morality and mortality is a fresh twist on the human condition. ... **Memortality** is one of those books that will incite more questions than it answers. And for fandom, that's a good thing."

— Ricky L. Brown, Amazing Stories

"Punchy and fast paced, **Memortality** reads like a graphic novel. ... (Provost's) style makes the trippy landscapes and mind-bending plot points more believable and adds a thrilling edge to this vivid crossover fantasy."

— Foreword Reviews

"The genres in this volume span horror, fantasy, and science-fiction, and each is handled deftly. ... **Nightmare's Eve** should be on your reading list. The stories are at the intersection of nightmare and lucid dreaming, up ahead a signpost ... next stop, your reading pile. Keep the nightlight on."

— R.B. Payne, Cemetery Dance

"**Memortality** by Stephen Provost is a highly original, thrilling novel unlike anything else out there."

— David McAfee, bestselling author of
33 A.D., 61 A.D., and 79 A.D.

"Profusely illustrated throughout, **Highway 99** is unreservedly recommended as an essential and core addition to every community and academic library's California History collections."

— California Bookwatch

"As informed and informative as it is entertaining and absorbing, **Fresno Growing Up** is very highly recommended for personal, community, and academic library 20th Century American History collections."

— John Burroughs, Reviewer's Bookwatch

"Provost sticks mostly to the classics: vampires, ghosts, aliens, and even dragons. But trekking familiar terrain allows the author to subvert readers' expectations. ... Provost's poetry skillfully displays the same somber themes as the stories. ... Worthy tales that prove external forces are no more terrifying than what's inside people's heads."

— Kirkus Reviews on **Nightmare's Eve**

"... an engaging narrative that pulls the reader into the story and onto the road. ... I highly recommend **Highway 99: The History of California's Main Street**, whether you're a roadside archaeology nut or just someone who enjoys a ripping story peppered with vintage photographs."

— Barbara Gossett,
Society for Commercial Archaeology Journal

THE ONLY DRAGON

Stephen H. Provost

The author writes about American highways, mutant superheroes, mythic archetypes and pretty much anything he wants. He spent 32 years working at daily newspapers in California as an editor, reporter and columnist. These days, he's a historian, philosopher and novelist with more than a dozen books to his credit. And he loves cats. Read his blogs and keep up with his latest activities at stephenhprovost.com.

Made in the USA
Middletown, DE
01 November 2022

13895514R00116